Retail Island

Christopher Nosnibor

Retail Island

First published 2018 by Clinicality Press

http://clinicalitypress.com

ISBN 978-0-9556939-7-7

By the same author

Bad Houses
C.N.N. (with Stuart Bateman)
THE PLAGIARIST
Postmodern Fragments
From Destinations Set
The Gimp
The Changing Face of Consumerism
This Book is Fucking Stupid
The Rage Monologues

This is a work of fiction. It is dedicated to two people in particular, who helped shape key characters.

Part 1: Arrivals

Arriving in any new job in an unknown city invariably brings with it a sense of dislocation and a need to reacclimatise, however accustomed one is to travel and life on the move. Robert Ashton arrived at the office of Medico Inc., York, calmly and serenely, having spent the last six years on projects at various locations away from his home on the outskirts of London. His arrival at the location had been comfortable and without hitch: while he often flew, York's accessibility on the North Coast Main Line meant that the city was a mere two hours by rail from King's Cross, a comfortable journey by First Class with food and beverages included on the company tab. He'd taken a taxi from the station to the out-of-town location of Ebor Park. The office was situated, along with many others, not beside a green expanse with lakes and trees, but on the peripheries of a large retail park, which also incorporated a brace of chain hotels.

As he climbed out of the taxi at around seven thirty in the evening, Robert mused on how the British retail park is a similar concept to the North American 'power center' which began its rise to prominence in the second half of the 1980s. The decade that gave rise to the new capitalism and global consumerism had not only changed the face of culture and society, but the geographical landscape, forever. While primarily constructed on brownfield sites and previously developed land, the fact that nature had begun to reclaim large swathes of space to create scrubby meadows on former industrial wasteland meant that green and brown had turned dark grey as mile upon mile of tarmac-surfaced car parks occupied ever greater expanses. Their march, it seemed, was far from over, and seasoned as he was to existing in such spaces, Robert couldn't help but marvel at the enormity – and the architectural bleakness – of Ebor Park.

Mapped out with retail units, including Boots, Burtons, WH Smith, New Look, Hobbycraft, and H&M, as well as refreshment outlets including Starbucks, Costa, and Pizza Hut, Ebor Park was the epitome of the cloned space, and Robert was immediately struck – and crushed – by its barren absence of character. Stashed in one corner, a twisted metal platform surrounded by wood chippings advertised itself as the 'magical tree garden'. Being neither magical nor a garden, its spartan steel sculpture-like structure bore only the vaguest resemblance to a tree. Its four-foot slide was beneath any child over eighteen months, and it existed as a monument to the most depressing realisations of contemporary consumer culture and twenty-first century childhood. Robert could have been anywhere, and equally felt like he was nowhere. This was not hell, but purgatory: Ashton found himself surrounded by the most anonymous renditions of all of the major chain stores he had yet to witness. The absence of soul was beyond tangible. Ebor Park was, in summary, death with air-conditioning and large hoardings, accompanied by a vast expanse of car park.

He checked in at the Travelodge which would be his home for the next six weeks while he worked on the project. He went through the usual on-arrival routine after a journey of length, first unpacking his suitcase into the anonymous, standard-issue wardrobe and drawers, before taking a shower and shaving. Dried, dressed, and refreshed, Robert cast an eye over the view that would be his for the foreseeable future. And the view was bleak. Flat roofs, plate glass shop fronts, and car parks dominated his vista.

It was around seven forty-five when Ashton returned to reception. "Where would you recommend for dinner?" he asked the receptionist.

"Well, most of our guests dine at the hotel's own restaurant," replied the anonymous, pale-faced man in uniform behind the desk.

Robert nodded, and indicated that he would like further options. He found the sameness of hotel dining rooms depressing, although similarly, chain dining outlets had an equally disorientating effect, in that it was impossible to differentiate one from another, and as such, impossible to retain a sense of location between the different cities.

"The retail park itself is closed now, but during the day it has a Pizza Hut, Costa, and Starbucks for light refreshments. At the phase two retail park, around ten to fifteen minutes away, there is a Nando's, Ed's Easy Diner, Prezzo, Frankie & Benny's, Giraffe Café, Wok 'n' Go, and they're all open to 9:30 or 10pm, and Caffe Nero is open till 8:30."

"How about pubs?"

"There is a pub, The Orchard Carvery, which offers carvery until 10pm, as well as a selection of local ales, which is very good. Huge portions, and really good value for money. That's around five minutes away if you're walking."

Robert opted for this final venue, despite having limited expectations of it actually being a real pub, or there being anything resembling a tree-bearing fruit within a three-mile radius. His low expectations were met on the discovery that it was a clone establishment, one of a growing number of purpose-built appendices to the retail park experience as devised by one of the major breweries. Still, he reflected, with the shops closed and it being after 'tea time' when tired shoppers tended to stuff their faces after long hours traipsing the aisles of New Look and Poundland, the place was quiet, and they did serve reasonable local beers at low prices.

Keen to escape the bright yellow-tinged artificial lighting and garish patterned carpet that rendered the venue a facsimile of a traditional pub, he didn't loiter after finishing his meal. Instead, Robert returned to his room to cast his eyes once more over his brief, which gave precious little away beyond the fact the project was highly confidential, before taking an early night.

****

Retail Island

Ashton's sparse and uninformative – yet perversely wordy – fifteen-page brief specified that he should arrive at reception of the office of Medico Inc. for 10am on Monday morning, and to ask for Jack Barham. Barham had proved to be a typical corporate male in his mid-forties: he was around five feet ten, sporting a tailored pinstripe navy suit, smart haircut, and the onset of middle-age spread well set without yet having reached obesity. The welcome committee was bolstered by a tall, slender brunette in a pencil skirt and whose ID card, which swung from the customary company lanyard around her neck, informed Robert that her name was Vicky Hoyle. Robert prickled a little as he felt Hoyle's hand on the back of his upper arm as she ushered him through the gate at reception and into the office proper. He had never been one for physical contact with strangers, acquaintances or colleagues, or even the majority of friends, and felt it to be an unwelcome encroachment into his personal space.

As Robert endured Jack's overbearing handshake and insincere grin, he couldn't help but observe the fact that Vicky – who smiled and nodded but spoke little – resembled an animated mannequin manufactured purely for the purpose of corporate promotional photos and videos. She had perfectly sculpted eyebrows and skin made for a cosmetics advertisement, and was conventionally attractive to the point of being an airbrushed amalgamation of attractive stereotypes: a bland, forgettable composite, and as such, impossible to forge an explicit attraction to.

"Welcome, welcome," Barham gushed as he pumped Robert's hand mechanically. Ashton took an immediate dislike to the man. No, dislike was perhaps rather strong. More specifically, he felt it would be impossible to bond or find commonality with a man so entrenched in embodying his corporate identity, whose character was so thickly veneered in characterless façade.

"Good to meet you," Robert nodded noncommittally.

Jack grinned and radiated an air of calculated dynamism. Vicky just smiled, a crisp, toothy smile that was as plastic and brittle as a vending-machine cup.

"So, we'll get you a pass sorted, Robert," Jack said.

"Are you Robert? Or Rob? Bob? Bobby?"

Robert winced silently at Barham's ingratiating and somewhat insolent patter. "Robert," he confirmed dryly. He'd have been Robert in Jack's presence regardless of his preferred form of address. He resisted the urge to ask if Jack was his given name, or a diminutive of James, John or Jacob, or if his interlocutor was just a prick.

"Sure, sure," Jack blustered. "If you could just sign in the book here, and take this temporary day pass for now, you should have a full contractor permit before the end of the day. That'll make you feel more at home. Then we'll take you on a tour of the facility and introduce you to the rest of the team who are on this project. Obviously, we've not really told you a great deal about the job yet... have they had you sign the NDA yet?"

"Yes," Robert affirmed. "It was inbuilt into the contract. So I'm effectively in the dark here."

"Good, good," Barham boomed bombastically as he opened the gate and led Robert into the office space behind the reception desk. "All will be revealed," he said, the combination of condescension and enigma grating immediately on his guest. "Although it will be in stages. Ordinarily, we like to hit the ground running, but on this one, rather than overloading you, we'll be operating in a more piecemeal way and on a need-to-know basis."

He led Robert through a succession of doors and corridors, Vicky keeping pace silently at Robert's side as if corralling him into position. Shepherded into a glass-walled meeting room with large flat screens and an array of telecoms equipment inbuilt into the expansive white table, which was surrounded by black leatherette chairs, Robert found himself being introduced to the majority of the other workers on the project. As usual, he forgot their names and functions as quickly as they were given. A plump, middle-aged woman with straw-blonde hair who chuckled a lot and talked unnecessarily about shoes and diets, seemingly in an attempt to deflect from the fact she had nothing of substance to contribute to the project; a fat bloke in his forties; another fat bloke in his fifties, balding and bored-looking; a thick-set guy whose shirt was too tight who rambled inanely and in autistic detail about nothing of consequence; a shrewish-looking woman of indeterminate age, with saggng breasts, and wearing a misshapen floral charity-shop dress; a woman in her early fifties displaying what seemed perhaps an inappropriate amount of cleavage; a woman in her late twenties or early thirties who spoke little but held herself well: these would be Robert's immediate colleagues for the duration of his stay, although Jack informed him that a number of absentees would also play major roles in the project.

Over the course of almost three hours, Robert learned precious little about the project itself, but a considerable amount about the ambitions of the company. Being a multinational pharma, they had their eye on global domination and were heavily involved in lobbying for compulsory vaccinations on every level. Although not expressed explicitly, it was clear they had transitioned beyond conventional marketing a considerable time ago and were now bent on infiltrating governments and media and would stop at nothing to achieve their objectives. The one thing that was rendered apparent during the course of the meeting was that this latest project was prospectively revolutionary, but these were the formative testing stages, and that given the nature of the tests, secrecy was of the utmost importance.

Robert began to feel uncomfortable, and began to wonder if he was being drawn into something that hinted at the MK Ultra project as his mind wandered during an extended fluff piece, replete with slide deck. *When did a PowerPoint presentation become a slide deck?* Robert wondered.

Watching Vicky cross and uncross her perfectly-proportioned legs, which were clearly waxed rather than shaved, he wondered if she was truly as lacking in character as she presented.

****

On walking into the office on Tuesday morning, Robert noticed the smell of breakfast – in particular bacon, sausages and fried eggs – drifting from the direction of the canteen. The smell turned his stomach. He wasn't much of a breakfast person at the best of times, and preferred a light start to his dietary day, with a piece of toast and a strong, black coffee. It was not quite seven thirty, and as he cursed the sadist who had booked a meeting for seven forty-five, he wondered if the canteen staff weren't a little previous in their preparations. What state would all of the pre-cooked food be in by the time the regular 9-5 workforce arrived?

The smell continued up the two flights of stairs to the landing, where he took a left and swiped his card a third time after the main doors and the turnstiles that separated reception from the main body of the building. He considered briefly the level of security in the building. The turnstiles meant that tailgating was extremely difficult, and wondered if the internal blocks to facilitate access to the individual wings wasn't overkill given that the rest of the office was vacant, making it unlikely anyone who wasn't an employee or contractor would be unlikely to be able to gain access and liberate confidential information.

Robert was surprised to see just how many people were already in the office and at their desks, or otherwise milling about in the kitchenette or making their way to the various meeting points; glass-walled rooms and clusters of settees and brightly-coloured poufs. A brief scan suggested as many as ten or fifteen percent of staff were already signed in.

He strolled to the hot-desking station he had been assigned the previous morning, placed his bag on the anonymous desktop, a brilliant white rectangle bereft of features save for an Internet docking port and a brace of mains sockets, and scanned the office in search of Jack Barham. Unable to locate him, he squinted around for Vicky Hoyle by way of an alternative, but wondered precisely how much help she would be. She'd yet to prove herself to be anything more than short-skirted wallpaper, and Robert wasn't entirely sure of her operational function, to use the type of business parlance he so detested.

Robert's success as a consultant was based upon his ability to 'cut through the treacle' as he'd seen some companies describe it, to 'blast through bullshit' as the edgier firms he'd worked with has pitched it, and to 'battle the bureaucracy' as others still had commented. And yet he felt, even in the early stages of this assignment, that he was battling against a wall of obfuscation. He still had yet to establish what the project entailed, and he was aware that six weeks was a short span, even with a full and detailed briefing, neither of which he had received as yet.

As if teleported into Robert's vicinity, Jack Barham suddenly appeared. He looked crisp, alert, more like a man playing the role of a sharp, go-getting exec in a big-budget US TV series than a real office worker.

"Robert, good morning!" he exclaimed confidently and with an energy and enthusiasm disproportionate to both the situation and the time of day.

"Morning Jack," Robert returned with a little less bonhomie. He was weary despite having slept well, and found himself feeling a shade of suspicion about his new colleague's demeanour.

"How was your first night's stay? Comfortable? I've heard nothing but good things about the Travelodge.'

"My second night, actually," Robert corrected, flatly, "and it was fine. Comfortable enough. I've stayed in a lot of big-chain hotels over the years. They do tend to blur after a while, and it's generally only the bad ones that really stand out. Still, absolutely no complaints so far."

"Good, good," Jack said, vaguely dismissively, as if Robert's improvised dialogue which extended beyond a bland affirmative or direct positive affirmation had interrupted his script. "I'm assuming you've had breakfast? So you're all set? Do you want to grab a coffee or some water or anything beforehand?"

"No, no, I'm fine, thank you,' Robert assured him.

"Ok, great. Well, I just need to go and grab a few bits and then we can make our way to the meeting room. You can get yourself set up here, or whatever, and I'll pop down and grab you on the way. Obviously, we're keen to get started on time."

"Obviously," echoed Robert. "I don't think I've ever seen an office this busy so early," he remarked spontaneously. "Aren't normal office hours nine to five?"

Jack looked surprised by this unexpected observation. "Well, yes, but we're all passionate here. No-one ever conquered the world by adhering to strict hours and clock-watching. It's all about going the extra mile."

"The staff here work long days, then?"

"Well, yes, the dedication of the staff is second to none. Twelve, thirteen-hour days are very much standard. The world doesn't stop turning outside of regular business hours. The nine to five is almost an irrelevance in a global market. It's a 24/7 culture, and if you snooze you lose."

Robert took particular exception to this phrase: he may have forged a career in industry and have spent a lifetime battling insomnia and other forms of sleep disturbance, even joking occasionally that 'sleep is the enemy', but something about rhyming corporate catchphrases really stuck in his craw. 'You snooze you lose' not only set a competitive benchmark of 'winners' and 'losers' but also advocated a culture of living to work, a lifestyle whereby all work and no play was the route to success, and even implied, against a backdrop of increasing emphasis on employee welfare and wellbeing, that in actual fact, sleep deprivation was encouraged in the quest for achievement. Robert knew all about sleep deprivation, and while his position as a traveling consultant was evidence of a certain degree of success, his sleep deprivation and its physically and psychologically detrimental effects had played no part in his achieving it.

****

Retail Island

The planned meetings ended early, and various members of the project team had a range of reasons to depart the office early on Tuesday afternoon. Consequently, Robert decided to take the opportunity to head into town. The woman in her late twenties or early thirties who spoke little but held herself well, who he learned was named Rebecca, offered to accompany him, and the woman in her early fifties who had displayed what seemed perhaps an inappropriate amount of cleavage, who her ID card identified as Fiona Dexter, accompanied them. Robert was unsure about the arrangement: while the former seemed genuine and sincere, the latter had a pushy edge and also seemed overly keen in some indefinable way.

The office itself had only limited parking, and the vast expanse of tarmac in the centre of Ebor Park was reserved strictly for those frequenting the retail outlets. With myriad CCTV cameras surveying every inch of the park, 'they' knew who was not visiting any of the stores, just as 'they' knew if anyone had been parked for more than the three-hour limit and was therefore subject to a fine. And so the best means of access to town or office from either point or any in between was via the shuttle bus, and Medico employees benefitted from being able to use the service for free. Medico even had its own sponsored bus-stop, located on the loop of road which served as a sort of mini-ring-road around the park, which was accessed by a sleek covered walkway which extended from the reception doors, past the decorative pond and borders, to the collection point. Everything about the architecture seemed designed to protect, or otherwise separate, the individuals from the outside world, to cosset, envelop, to construct a hermetic world apart from the humdrum hubbub of not only the park, but the rest of the city and society at large.

Robert, Rebecca, and Fiona stood and waited for the bus and chatted about little in particular. Robert was still very much on guard, and was also waiting to see if either of these colleagues revealed greater depths. He'd been in the game long enough to know it was foolish to be the first to reveal one's hand and was equally aware that the people he was working with may simply have no depths to reveal, which meant that any efforts on his part were futile.

While his wife was wholly unaware of this, Robert had discovered this the hard way, and had found himself in compromising positions of disclosure quite by accident in the past.

On the arrival of the bus, Rebecca bade them farewell, heading for her car parked some distance away on a car-park subsidised by Medico, and on embarking, Fiona positioned herself at the very front and buried her head in a Sudoku game on her tablet, making it abundantly clear that she did not wish to interact further. Robert took no issue with this, preferring to observe his colleagues' natural default behaviours over a false attempt to forge a friendship. That said, a small part of him felt wounded that no-one felt any desire to make any attempt to offer any kind of company given his status as a lone visitor. In fact, he would later reflect in his hotel room that the lack of support, guidance and general hospitality was rather unusual. These people responsible for the creation and provision of medical supplies were, it seemed, clinical to the point of borderline brutality.

The bus itself sounded alive, popping with the crackle of three dozen shopping bags, all bulging with plus-size skinny-cut jeans and size eighteen elasticated leggings and lycra vests, T-Shirts, diaphanous blouses and gypsy tops for the summer.

It had been barely two full days, but Robert was beginning to feel a growing rift between Medico and the outside world, and was beginning to feel a certain sense of confusion as the two gravitational pulls exerted their force on his being. Much as he felt disconnected and at odds with post-millennial culture at large, he felt a sense of unease about the culture which seemingly permeated Medico. It was something he couldn't readily define. Instead of troubling his already crowded mind on it in the moment, he elected, after a psychogeographical meandering of the city's main streets, to hunker down in a pub – the upstairs room of a hidden gem by the name of Pivni – with the paperback novel he'd brought with him – a battered copy of Michel Houellebecq's *Atomised* – and to clear his mind before morning.

****

By Thursday, Robert was growing frustrated, and this was manifesting itself as a restless unease. Something, he felt, was not quite right. He was well accustomed to signing non-disclosure agreements in his line of work: the world of pharmaceuticals, like the government and military, and like finance, was clandestine by its nature. But the fact a condition of the contract was that he would sign an NDA before even agreeing to work the project, and having been left in the dark even on arrival at the office struck him as unusual. Moreover, he felt he was wasting his time: the majority of his time since his arrival had been spent observing how various departments operated.

On Wednesday, Robert had been invited to a meeting with some of the marketing managers. The meeting had been initiated by a woman named Fay Hunter. 'Our wing of the office is a bit of a maze,' she'd said on the phone, so if you'd like me to come and meet you at reception...' Robert had accepted the offer, despite the fact he usually preferred to stroll the corridors of offices anonymously and make his own way to designated locations. He considered it a sign of weakness to have someone hold his hand to guide him around, and actively enjoyed the opportunity to explore, even though one sterile corporate environment very much resembled another.

And so it was that he was sitting in reception when a woman in her late twenties or early thirties rushed in, harried and breathless, glancing around in search of a face that might belong to a Robert Ashton, consultant. She greeted him and introduced herself as Fay: they shook hands before she led him through a labyrinth to a hidden wing of the complex. He was immediately struck by how much more cheaply decorated this part of the office was in comparison to the executive areas he had spent his time thus far. The meeting room was small, a flimsy construction of frosted glass walls and plate glass door, a far cry from the plush suites with hessian-textured wallpaper and lined with abstract art, secluded from the world outside by thick wooden doors which offered complete soundproofing.

As much as anything, Robert was curious to understand the mechanisms of the organisation, how the different echelons of the staff connected, and how they would feed into the project he still knew practically nothing about. But equally, he found himself curious about Fay: she was a slim, attractive brunette with pale skin and blue eyes; well-proportioned, and with shoulder-length hair, her demeanour was reserved, but not shifty, and he suspected she had hidden depths beneath her subtly sarcastic disposition.

Robert, by nature, had a tendency to study people, and he was intrigued by both the geometry of her face and the contours of her breasts, firm and full, pressing against the fabric of her tight white blouse.

The meeting itself was enlightening, in that it revealed to Robert just how extreme the segregation between the levels of staff was. The front-line staff hadn't the slightest inkling of what the company was actually planning, or the products they were developing, or had already brought to market.

"To be honest," Fay intimated, "Most of the front-line staff are more concerned with paying the bills than with ethics. They're simply contact centre staff. Medical trials don't interest them. What they're interested in is the new Primark that's opening a week on Saturday."

"That huge space on the corner of the retail park?"

"Yes. It's a big deal. I think it'll bring a lot more people out here."

"Christ. It's busy enough already. What about the town centre?"

"Parking in the city centre's awful. The streets are narrow and the place gets packed out with tourists, especially at weekends. Out of town shopping is what people prefer now. And most of the people who work here are happy to have more shops at the retail park, because they can't get into town during the week."

"And what do they do at weekends?"

"More of the same, mostly" Fay said.

"How depressing. Shopping and work: the new opium of the people."

"Yes, something like that. But there are a few things I could show you that might be of interest if you're looking for something to do, and I'm not talking about tourism."

Her delivery didn't carry so much as the vaguest hint of a come-on, and so Robert took it at face value.

"It's a shame pharmaceutical companies like Medico can't find a cure for apathy," Ashton said archly.

Hunter looked him straight in the eyes, an unguarded expression of surprise on her face for a fleeting moment. She didn't speak, but instead wrote something on the bottom of her note pad. Then she tore off a strip and handed it to Robert: he saw it was her phone number. "I can't really talk here, but text me and I can tell you."

Wednesday ended with what was pitched as a routine daily debriefing with Jack Barham. Jack spoke circuitously around matters of funding and projected completion dates, and Robert found himself becoming increasingly bored, but noticed Barham repeatedly touching Vicky Hoyle's knee as she sat next to him, stilted, robotic, and passive to the point of near-invisibility, a personality vacuum.

"There is one thing," he said, interrupting Barham's spiel.

"What's that?"

"This project. I still haven't received any details whatsoever. It feels like I'm being enlisted to work for MI5."

"Funny you should say that," Jack said, a serious expression on his face. "Did you read the NDA?"

"Most of it," Robert confessed. He felt as though he had entered an eternal loop of forgetfulness, and found himself growing tense with frustration at being asked the same questions and making no obvious progress. "I accept the principles of any NDA. But on this occasion, well, I can't disclose information I'm not party to. And as it stands, I have no information whatsoever."

"It's very much operating on a need-to-know basis," Barham agreed.

"But surely I need to know," Robert contested.

"And you will. But only what you need to know. And what you need to know you'll find out in the meeting we've got booked for tomorrow morning."

Robert spent the rest of the afternoon holed up in a corner of the canteen, engaged in independent research. Something about Medico struck him as unusual, not least of all the casual and liberal air of sex and sexism, as he witnessed a number of men grab, stroke and rub female colleagues in overtly inappropriate ways. It did, however, seem to operate in both directions, as he saw a woman approach the desk of a man who was engaged in a teleconference and, without warning, stroked his beard, and another sidle up to a man waiting by one of the coffee machine and casually rub her breasts against his back, before reaching around and squeezing his crotch.

There was no apparent or overt context, and Ashton simply found himself confused by these physical exchanges, noting their entirely non-verbal nature.

****

Retail Island

The meeting ran for a full five and a half hours, with half an hour out for lunch, during which time the delegates adjourned to the canteen. There was a steady flow of human traffic to the counter, with employees refueling on soup, jacket potatoes, prepacked sandwiches, and various permutations of overcooked stodge with chips. But as the delegates sat chatting, mindful to avoid the topic of their coming together outside the soundproof, air-conditioned confines of the meeting room, in a space where the rank and file may overhear them, Robert noticed just how few of the workers made use of the seating area in the canteen. Despite being a large space, with tables accompanied by four to six chairs, sufficient to accommodate at least seventy-five in all, there were rarely more than three or four other people dining in at any given time.

Robert had been hungry, and so had opted for the lasagne with chips. Working his way through the sloppy, salty-yet-bland pasta dish and undercooked potato product, he began to appreciate why his colleagues had chosen self-service salads, seeded granary baguettes, and bottled smoothies. The food made him feel as uncomfortable as the looks some of the other delegates gave him as he ate.

"Did you miss breakfast?" asked a burly, bearded man named Tom Grindstaff. His attempt at humour carried a needlingly sarcastic edge.

"I was just hungry," replied Robert, trying not to sound defensive.

"I know it's a cliché," Jack chipped in as he sipped on the green sludge that clung to the inside of a plastic bottle, "but I treat my body as a temple. Since I turned 35, I just realised that I wasn't getting any younger, and that it's important to look after yourself."

"Same here," concurred Steve Johnson, a tall man in a navy pinstripe suit who sported a short beard, trimmed at the neck and who wore his receding fringe flicked into a stiffly-gelled quiff. "I tried clean eating for a while, but that was a bit too extreme, and difficult to manage. Besides, I enjoy beer too much to be really strict. Vegansim was never going to work for me because I love meat. But I only have organic meat now, and it has to be lean, and I limit it to three or four days a week, and I have one day a week on juicing, and a weekly vitamin C flush, too. But I took up cycling, and I run around eight K daily. I drink at least two litres of water a day and only drink alcohol on weekends. I've got so much more energy, my complexion has improved and my BMI is now twenty-five, when it was twenty-seven point nine three years ago."

"It's definitely about finding a regime that suits you," Tom nodded sagely. "But yes, hydration and exercise are key. Plenty of cardio. I do an hour in the office gym before work every morning."

"Even today?" asked Robert.

"How you mean?" Steve queried.

"The early start... the seven-thirty meeting..."

"That isn't an early start. I'm always in the gym for six and at my desk for seven twenty. I work till seven or eight in the evening, have a light meal and am in bed for ten to ten thirty."

"All work..." began Robert.

"I love my work, it's better and far more rewarding than any play," Jack pontificated.

By the end of the meeting, Robert felt he had learned little, other than that his comment about MI5 had perhaps been more accurate than he would have given credit. Ultimately, he felt vaguely surplus to requirement, and a growing edginess was embedding itself in his psyche.

"So, what exactly are these drugs we're producing and promoting?" Robert asked, prickling slightly. "I need to get this straight. The pitch is that they're a range of breakthrough anti-depressants, and anti-psychotics, but in fact they're the precise opposite: pro-depressants, pro-psychotics?"

"That's a very reductive description," Jack intoned. His expression made clear that the conversation was over.

****

Robert's next appointment was a workshop led by Rebecca Beckham, whom he had met on the first day. He wasn't entirely sure of her function either before or after, but she did show the session's attendees a number of complex graphs and graphics on an extensive slide deck.

The bulk of her remit, it appeared, was to explain the psychology of sales, and to put forward a theory about how pharmaceuticals – particularly inoculations – promoted a general sense of wellbeing in the border populace.

She had long, mid-brown hair and pleasant, passive features. She wore her thick-rimmed designer glasses up on the top of her head, and was dressed in a stereotypically business-like fashion, with a plain, mid-grey knee-length skirt and a silvery blouse which had a shiny, silken finish. A facsimile of a corporate worker, she spoke confidently and convincingly, but Robert would later reflect on how the majority of her script was devoted to empty corporate speak and second-generation psychobabble.

Of the nine others present, Robert only recognized the bland-looking Phil Thompson, and Janice Smythe, a young woman with over-teased ash-blonde hair and a stern expression that bordered on sour. Robert had had only limited contact with either, and did not feel comfortable initiating conversation. Smythe emanated a sense of superiority, and Thompson seemed detached, aloof, and uninteresting.

During the group exercises, which required the workshop's participants to separate into groups of three or four to complete specific task and exercises, Rebecca would move between the groups and ask how they were getting on and enquire about their methodologies. Robert noticed how she would confidently, and seemingly knowingly, lean forward and reveal her cleavage to her colleagues. At one point, she sat beside Richard and sat at a quite unnatural angle which made it almost impossible for him not to notice the gape of her low-fronted blouse. She wore a half-cup push-up bra which her small breasts barely filled, leaving a visible space in which her small, stiff nipple could easily be seen, and she made a point of leaning over the notes the participants had made, nonchalantly but clearly knowingly facilitating glimpses of her pert assets.

During the mid-session break, Robert made his way to the gents' lavatories. Grunts and squeaks echoed from the second cubicle, and Robert strove to push erotic images from his mind in order to maintain a steady stream through a soft shaft. It wasn't, he pondered, that he found the idea of sexual activity in such proximity in itself arousing, so much as the fact that arousal was an instinctive reaction to what was, in essence, live pornography. His penis spasmed as he shook the last droplets of urine from his tip, and as he stuffed his thickening rod back into his fly, Robert heard a loud cracking, splintering sound, accompanied by a loud shriek and a gasp from the cubicle.

Retail Island

As he washed his hands, he saw the cubicle door open and a petite blonde in a minidress which she was pulling down over her thighs emerged. She tugged at its front to cover a slipped nipple and tried to look nonchalant, despite her hair being tousled and her cheeks aglow. Behind her, a tall, broad man with dark hair and dense, low eyebrows lumbered out. He wore a crumpled Transformers T-shirt and smeared glasses, and had crusted ejaculate visible around the bulging fly of his loose-cut black jeans. Pushing his steamed lenses back up his nose and brushing his greasy fringe back from his face, he wore an expression that was simultaneously dazed and self-satisfied. Glancing without thinking toward the cubicle, the splintering and shrieking made sense as he noticed the bowl of the lavatory was missing a large piece of porcelain. Seeing the ruddy cheeks of the guy in the Transformers T-Shirt, Robert tried his best to push the image from his mind.

Robert returned to the room where the workshop was being held to find the first segment of the second half was being presented by Steve Johnson. The other attendees had yet to return, so Robert sat quietly, biding his time and took the opportunity to check his emails and text messages on his phone. He could see that Johnson was psyching himself up, pacing the room and shaking his shoulders while chatting with Rebecca. Ashton's attention was drawn when Johnson stood still at the head of the table and emitted an empowering exhalation of air, pumping his fists simultaneously. He proceeded to unbuckle his belt and unzip his fly, flipping out his semi-erect penis.

Janice Smythe returned to the room and sat down, her face glued to her phone and seemingly oblivious as Johnson slowly and casually masturbated his stiffening shaft. As the others began to slowly filter in, he wiped a glistening pearl of pre-cum from his angry red tip with the palm of his hand, tucked his pulsating cock back into his trousers and rezipped before commencing his walkthrough of some Powerpoint slides on input, output, and throughput.

****

The office's chemistry provided a source of fascination as Robert whiled away many long hours wondering how to fill his time. In between reading around the various reports on strategy he had been passed, and browsing for reports on Medico and their operational methodology, he found himself contemplating the sexual dynamics of the workplace. Something about the office workspace was in itself erotic to a certain extent, albeit in an abstract sense. The crisp, linear clinicality of the office space, despite its open plan, seemed to gleam with erotic potential based around a sense of wrongness and incongruity. Another factor was the austerity of the requisite work attire: this somehow had the opposite of the desired effect, namely in that rather than providing an asexual uniformity, the suit, the skirt, the shirt, the blouse, seemed to accentuate physical aspects in a semi-unobtainable light, likely to create both a mystique and a certain frisson. This was common to many working environs. But while one would likely expect pockets of sexual tension in any office, Medico seemed to practically steam and crackle with pheromones and musk. Perfect strangers engaged in casual acts of frotteurism and Toucherism as Robert noticed colleagues subtly and not-so-subtly making physical contact, brushing past one another in tight spaces, even overtly making excessive and unnecessary contact while passing in corridors. Kraft Ebbing would have had a field day observing the interactions as groins surreptitiously rubbed against buttocks, hands swept against hips and breasts brushed backs and chests.

Ordinarily, these behaviours were merely alluded to in the workplace. At Medico, there was nothing simmering or beneath the surface: the kinks were rampant and rife. Was it something in the air – or the air-conditioning – which provoked this endless demonstration of sexual psychopathies and perverse paraphilias?

****

Friday was spent largely between meetings and surveying spreadsheets. Robert was struggling to settle, and his focus wasn't as sharp as it perhaps ought to have been. Increasingly, the entire setup of Medico, not just the project itself, was beginning to nag at him on numerous and seemingly unconnected levels. The operatives on the project – Project Mushroom, as it was in fact known – had been divided into cells, each charged with a specific task with regards to its strategy and execution. Because of the clandestine nature of the project, it had been determined that segmenting it, meaning that no one individual would be in possession of all of the facts, would limit the security risks.

By lunchtime, Robert's frustration was again beginning to mount, but also his suspicion. His question about Project Mushroom being about pro-psychotics had not been a facetious one, and Jack Barham's reaction to it suggested that he had hit rather too close to home. His mind was swimming with conjecture and confusion around the company's motivations and objectives, and these thoughts were underpinned by a sense of unease about the culture Medico seemed to espouse. Something about many of the staff and their behaviours struck Ashton as being strange, although beyond the blatant and unbridled sexuality, precisely how this strangeness manifested itself eluded him. And then there was Fay Hunter. Although she'd said little, something about what she had implied intrigued him, and he was also curious about her decision to hand him her number in the way she had.

Seeing Fay was on-line on the internal instant messenger, he sent a brief missive asking if she'd had her lunch break yet, and if she had no plans, if she felt like meeting up. She replied immediately, telling him to meet her in reception in fifteen minutes.

"Where shall we go?" asked Robert on arrival. "Costa? The Orchard Carvery?"

"Call me paranoid," Fay said, her pale lips pinched, "but I fear walls have ears. Walk with me."

Robert did as he was bid, and followed her to the off-site car park subsidised by Medico, where her white Toyota Aygo was parked. *En route*, she chatted animatedly about nothing in particular, and asked Robert about his background and his route to this particular contract. Robert felt unusually at ease with Fay, and noted that her pallid skin was punctuated across the bridge of her nose by small freckles. He couldn't help but study her features, her well-proportioned lips and even teeth as she spoke.

"Hop in," she smiled on reaching her car.

Robert slipped into the vehicle and strapped himself in. "Where are we going?" he asked.

"Nowhere," Fay replied. "I mean, we're just going to drive, not that we're going to sit in the car park," she added with a smile.

Her wry humour appealed to Robert, who smiled back as she put the car in gear and anxiously reversed out of the space.

"I'm sorry, I'm a really terrible driver," she apologised needlessly.

"You're fine," Robert reassured her as they exited the roundabout that led away from the retail park. "You haven't killed me yet."

Fay laughed. "There's plenty of time yet."

"So," Robert levelled. "What's going on at Medico?"

"I'll be honest," Fay replied, shaking her long dark hair and pulling a serious expression, "I don't really know. But recently I've started to feel something's not right."

"How do you mean?" Robert quizzed.

"It's hard to say... and I don't know why I'm telling you. Sometimes, I feel like I'm going nuts, and it's probably just paranoia. I do get paranoid, I'm a real worrier and probably a bit sensitive, but you know how you sometimes just sense something in your gut? But I feel like I can trust you," Fay confided.

"I'm an outsider, so you can probably trust me more because I've no vested interest and nothing really to gain through manipulation," Robert reassured her.

"I think that's probably it," she nodded. "There's something in the air, is all. It's like there's a tension in the office, something funny. I can't place it. It's like it's coming through the aircon or something. The atmosphere's changed and people are acting weirdly. Weird sex shit. I sort of need to be able to show you, but you need to be looking out for it first. Does that make any sense? You probably think I'm mad now," she added with a hint of reticence.

"Not at all," Robert said. Her edginess convinced him of her sincerity. "And I've already seen more than enough."

"It's not just the office," she added. "The retail park is weird, too."

"How so?"

"I'm not sure. But I'm sure it's not just me being paranoid."

"I notice there's a distinct lack of any kind of entertainment outlet, other than gaming," Robert said, changing the direction of their conversation slightly. "WH Smith have a limited selection of books, strictly bestsellers and leading genres – a large crime section, cookery, biographies, and there's an even smaller range of books in Asda. But there are very few magazines and no record shops or anything of the kind."

"But Robert, why would there be? No-one purchases entertainment in physical formats any more. Magazines are going out of print and print media has been in sharp decline for years now, and as for music and film... CD and DVD are practically obsolete. People stream film and music on-line and read their books on electronic devices. Where have you been?"

Robert shifted uncomfortably, suddenly feeling like a complete dinosaur, also struck by the use of his name. "I've been living in the world," he replied a fraction tersely, "but there are pockets of people who actually like physical media. Vinyl sales have been regaining ground recently, so while CDs have fallen from favour..."

"Yes, I know. But it's a blip, a fad. This place isn't simply about the now, it's the future. In the future – the near future – there will be no physical media. Digital is where it's at. Everything will be digital, everything will be automated. You can't not have noticed that the number of supermarket checkouts have been cut dramatically in favour of self-service. People prefer not to have to deal with people, or at least transact with them. Plus, fewer cashiers to pay help keeps costs down – or profits up. Everyone's after a bargain, especially in the age of austerity, now the money's run out. As I said, digital is the future.

On-line sales are already overtaking high-street sales. The high street is dead, Robert."

"Doesn't that completely negate the need for a place like this? Undermine its entire purpose?"

"Not at all, my friend." Fay beamed at this.

Robert squinted at her questioningly, but got no reply.

"It's all about the ritual. People love to shop. They still like to go and look at clothes, feel the fabric, try on shoes. The retail experience is an integral part of our culture. People need it. Click and collect means they get the best of both: the supermarket experience – actually being in the store – without all of the time spent traipsing the aisles."

"You're in the wrong line of work," said Robert. "Ever considered social sciences?"

Suddenly, Fay's expression changed and her jaw clenched. "We should get back."

"Of course."

Wheeling the car around back towards the retail park at the next roundabout, Fay surprised Robert by resting her hand on his knee. He thought better of commenting, and they spoke little on the final leg of their journey. On parking the little runaround, they climbed out and looked earnestly at one another.

"We should do this again sometime," said Robert lightly.

Fay nodded stiffly, an unequivocal affirmative, her jaw set and expression serious. "Yes, we should."

****

Retail Island

Robert indulged in a lie-in until after nine in the morning on Saturday, and took a leisurely shower and shave before taking a bus into the city to take in some of the tourist sites. While many in his position tended to take taxis which they billed as expenses, Robert preferred to go native when outside working hours. Besides, he simply didn't feel the need to charge for what were effectively leisure pursuits: that he got to travel on someone else's budget, and didn't have to pay for accommodation or meals had always seemed like a more than reasonable deal to him. He mused fleetingly over the long working hours the people at the office undertook, and how he had enjoyed career success in spite of his steadfast refusal to make the sacrifices espoused by most who achieved higher salary positions.

Initially, he was amazed by just how quiet it was, and ambulated the streets freely, taking in both The Shambles and Stonegate in unexpected peace. Near the Minster, the ferocity of the wind took him by surprise, and Ashton contemplated briefly the effect of the geography upon the microclimate in the vicinity.

Before long, the streets grew busy, but, he noticed, the majority of those ambling round were obviously tourists too, with large groups of Japanese visitors, led by flag-lofting tour guides, moving in procession and weaving past milling Americans and Germans lofting their iPads and digital SLR cameras in the direction of every old building in site.

By lunchtime, several trainloads of shaven-headed men from the north-east had descended on the city. Wearing a uniform of stonewashed comfort-fit jeans and shirts or t-shirts that pulled tight over their tattood arms and beer guts, they traversed the streets between the various sports bars and pubs in large groups, talking and laughing loudly and loutishly. Stag and hen parties, too, were getting under way, and Robert began to feel a little uncomfortable.

Taking refuge in Waterstones, which offered a disappointingly small selection of books in proportion to the amount of shelving units devoted to greetings cards and stationery, and the Costa coffee which occupied almost a quarter of the total floorspace. Robert took advantage of the space to browse at leisure.

There were a couple of clusters of mothers with pushchairs, and a middle-aged man in a green corduroy jacket, sipping cappuccinos, in the café, and one or two elderly people browsing the crime and romance sections, but otherwise the store was devoid of patrons. Robert was surprised by just how quiet it was. He appreciated the opportunity to scan the shelves without being jostled. Among the endless rows of run-of-the-mill mainstream potboilers and classics republished with slick new covers bearing either some quotation proclaiming the book's essential nature, or a glossy reproduction of the poster of the latest film adaptation, he was pleased to find a copy of JG Ballard's *Cncrete Island*, which he purchased, as much out of a sense of duty as a need for another volume to stow on the bookcase at home.

Robert commented on how quiet it was to the girl on the checkout, a willowy-looking studenty type with long brown hair streaked on one side with candyfloss pink.

"It's often quiet," she told him with a vague shrug of resignation.

"Even on a Saturday?"

"Especially on a Saturday. During the week, people from the offices in town come in, usually just to browse, for something to do during lunch, but they buy birthday cards and notebooks mostly when they do buy anything. But at weekends, all the shops are pretty much dead. Town is just tourists and stag and hen dos. The tourists are here for the sights and Betty's, the parties come for the booze. And everyone wants food. The cafés, restaurants, and fast-food outlets all do well, they're always busy."

"I thought we were a nation of shoppers," Robert remarked, punningly.

"Oh, we are," said the girl, smiling a little. "It's just that no-one comes into town to shop. We've got two major out-of-town retail parks and a designer outlet, which is a huge arcade. An indoor high street."

"So they can park their cars, walk a few yards and shop for hours without worrying about what the weather's doing when they're between shops."

"Exactly. It's climate-controlled, they can wear shorts and flip-flops all year round."

"The shopping equivalent of Centre Parcs?"

The girl laughed. "Yes, I suppose so. A shopping trip the weather can't spoil."

There was a cough from behind Robert, and he and the bookseller turned to see an elderly woman standing, holding a birthday card and looking irritated.

"I haven't got all day," she grouched.

Retail Island

The girl apologised and Robert thanked her before making a hasty exit, tucking his paperback into his coat pocket as he went.

Back out in the street, Robert began to feel hungry. As he wandered aimlessly, deliberating over the type of food he might want to eat, he was amazed by the sheer number of cafes, bistros, gastro-pubs, sushi bars, cake and ice cream parlours, bakeries, and other food outlets. He was also struck by the large number of vacant premises, of convenience stores – Tesco Metro, Sainsbury's Local, Morrisons – phone repair shops, and, by comparison, the relatively small number of actual retail outlets. The girl in the book shop had been right: the multitudinous eateries were heaving. The queues outside the multiple branches of Greggs, Thomas the Baker, and Coopland's Bakeries were immense. Subway was teaming, as, predictably, was McDonald's. The pubs, too, were packed, and after inching his way into three or four hostelries in search of a table, to be confronted by herds of obese people shovelling gargantuan portions down their gullets, Robert felt his appetite diminish. Instead, he took a stroll along a section of the city wall and admired the views.

****

The heavy breathing Robert heard on walking into the gents' was not the common, if somewhat disturbing, sound of someone defecating hard. The low grunts were parried at an equal, rhythmic pace by higher, breathier, squeaks which were unmistakably female. It was 8:03 on Monday morning, and Robert was feeling inexplicably weary. The gasp and grunt registered awkwardly with him, largely on account of the context, and the scene he had witnessed before the weekend returned to his mind. In a cultural climate where sexual liberation had seemingly been replaced by a clampdown on sexual malpractice, with no-one between the highest echelons of Hollywood and the Houses of Parliament above scrutiny, what seemingly passed as normal everyday conduct for Medico employees seemed beyond incongruous and struck Ashton as being ultimately immoral and disturbing.

Battling against himself, he continued about his business feigning oblivion, urinating with his eyes closed, and focusing his mind on the song playing in his head – quite inexplicably, 'Rowche Rumble' by The Fall. He exhaled silently, shook and zipped before making his way to the basin. As he soaped his hands, Robert caught sight of a movement in his peripheral vision in the mirror before him. In the shower cubicle, the door of which was less ajar than open by almost a foot, a woman in her mid to late twenties, with long, peroxide blonde hair which cascaded to the middle of her tanned back, was panting, her legs wrapped around the waist of a slightly rough-looking and heavy-set older guy. With his trousers pulled down around his ankles and his eyes closed in a near-climax grimace, Robert took a while to recognise the male as Jack Barham.

In the mirror, Ashton saw her climb down and turn around, angling her pelvis so that Barham could re-enter her from behind. The girl's breasts were immense, and judging by their limited movement and upward point, probably fake; her mahogany nipples were stretched to well over two inches in diameter and her face and body were a deep, unnatural dun hue.

"Fuck me," she panted in a thick northern accent. Her massive cans jiggled awkwardly as the man pumped his pelvis harder and faster.

"I'm fucking you," was the reply.

"Fuck me," she gasped again.

"I'm so close," he replied. "So close. Can you feel that?"

"I can feel it.... Oh, oh. I can feel you fucking me. I can feel your hot cock. Fucking me. Yeah, fuck me. Fucking shoot it in me, ya big-cocked bastard."

"I'm fucking coming, you whore. Can you feel me coming?"

"Yes. Just fucking shoot it in me, you fucking bastard."

"I'm coming. I'm coming so fucking hard. I want to come on your tits. Your fucking massive tits."

"Come on then, you bastard. Come on my tits."

Robert realized he had been washing his hands for the best part of three minutes as he watched on in the reflective surface, and saw Jack Barham again withdraw his stubby cock from between the girl's glistening vulva. She knelt down before him and lashed her tongue over his circumcised penis like it was a fast-melting ice lolly. She moaned crazily and he emitted a long, slow sigh of satisfaction.

There was nothing subtle or romantic about the scene: this was pure desperation, an urgent and depraved fuck, hurried and needful. Barham shot his load furiously, streaming his spunk over her colossal spherical wabs. They both trilled at the ejaculation, and he immediately planted his face is her immense cleavage, rubbing his nose, mouth, chin, and forehead in the sperm running down her tight, tanned skin. A look of idiotic delight traversed his face as he motorboated the jugs, each one as big as his head.

Seconds later, he was on his knees, his face buried in her snatch, furnished with a classically porny, if slightly dated, Brazilian. He lapped frantically at her distended lips, and she was far from restrained in her reaction.

Ashton realised he'd been standing at the basin transfixed for far too long. He was not a voyeur by nature, but this was compelling viewing. It wasn't that he was unfamiliar with the world of the office tryst, but this was something else altogether. It was so brazen, and they behaved as if it was so normal.

He felt vaguely sick as he finished rinsing the foam from his hands and wrists in scalding hot water.

****

Following his witnessing of this sordid encounter, Robert found himself freshly attuned to the sexual friction which seemingly pervaded the Medico office. To state that the workplace 'crackled' with tension would be as cliché as misstated: it was something altogether different that Ashton found himself observing. It was as if all of the employees were openly groping one anther when they stopped by one another's desks or stood waiting at the drinks machines. This wasn't the case, although some very much were. Moreover, he had become very quickly and very acutely aware of the nature of many of the comments which passed between colleagues. What struck him as curious was the fact that his was not conventional office sleaze, the occasional guy still yet to progress from the 1970s making remarks no longer deemed acceptable in the post-millennial workplace, but a culture based on a mutual exchange of dialogue that could only be considered, at least to an outsider as simply 'wrong'.

Noting that Fay was out of the office, he took the initiative she had steered him towards and sent her a text message; without divulging any detail, he intimated that he thought the atmosphere at Medico was beyond unusual, and if this was what she'd been referring to when they spoke, then they should perhaps meet.

Retail Island

She replied within minutes, saying she was busy today but suggesting lunch the following day. Robert accepted. On doing so, he felt a small and unexpected prickle of excitement. There was something about Fay that drew him.

****

Finding himself at a loose end at lunch, and feeling a strong urge to escape the confines of the office, Robert excused himself from the standing invitation to accompany Jack Barham, Steve Johnson, and Tom Grindstaff, along with any other taggers-along, to the canteen. More often than not, the core trio were accompanied by one or more culled from a selection of Nancy Leg, a petite bespectacled blonde who did a line in short dresses and worked in finance; Phil Thompson, an anonymous-looking, thick-set man in his thirties or forties who was heavily into rugby league; Janice Smythe, who worked on a fixed-term contract in HR and who took every opportunity to turn conversation to design and animal welfare; Samantha Bertram, a tall woman in her mid-thirties who worked in the legal department, who Robert couldn't help but notice possessed a substantial rack which he pitched at a DD, and John Cockram from marketing, whom Robert pegged as an irritating and vacuous hipster. While he found the atmosphere at The Orchard Carvery depressing on account of the ageing clientele, slobbering into their grey-looking carvery meals, not to mention the council estate mums with their rowdy kids, and the dismal shoppers laden with bags from Asda and New Look, Robert still found comfort in the solitude of a quiet corner with a panino and a pint. Medico's policy on the consumption of alcohol during working hours was vague – a fact which didn't surprise Robert in the slightest given his experience thus far – and besides, as a consultant, his ultimate take on the matter was 'fuck it'. Retiring to a two-seater table away from the bar with a pint of Yankee's Rooster and the copy of *Concrete Island* he had brought with him, Robert felt the tension which had been building slowly dissipate. He fleetingly pondered how different – and yet how similar – Ballard's later works were from his earlier ones, before returning his thoughts to Project Mushroom, about which he still knew so little.

What was it about this assignment, he asked himself, that caused him so much anxiety? Because, he realised uncomfortably, that he was actually beginning to feel almost constantly anxious about the whole thing. This in itself troubled him: Robert Ashton was not an anxious man by nature. But something about this place...

The fact that Project Mushroom was set to launch on Saturday gnawed away at him. Moreover, the fact the project he had been called in to act as a consultant on, but which he felt he knew practically nothing about and was being kept in the dark over, was set to launch without his even being fully aware of its objectives, let alone its full remit, gnawed away at him even more.

Robert took a long, slow, sip of his beer and he considered his position. He very much felt like a mushroom right now. He probably ought not care: they were paying him around a thousand pounds a day for his input and he was paid regardless of how much input he actually provided.

At the next table, an obese Scotsman on crutches and wearing cropped cargo pants, a T-shirt and flip-flops complained to his equally obese wife how busy it was, and how it had been busy on every occasion they had visited. "Still, no' a bad table, heh? Did ye get enough turkey in there?"

"Aye. No' as theck as ah'd've liked et, but…"

"Aye. But for three ninety-five, et's no' bad, ye get an alright sandwich an' a bet o' salad."

"Aye."

****

Friday brought with it the usual round of check-ins, walk-throughs of graphs and charts, and lengthy discussions on strategy which were couched in coded terminologies, and even the most highly specific details were delivered with an obfuscating vagueness. Robert began to wonder if any of the project operatives actually knew what they were talking about, or if there even was a project. And yet he was also increasingly conscious of his own growing unease: his heart was beginning to palpate each time he entered a meeting, and an air of apprehension hung over him almost constantly. Not being the anxious type, this was unfamiliar territory.

Mid-afternoon, he had a teleconference to dial into, and had been given a room from which to make the call.

On entering the room, he was surprised to find Fiona Dexter and Samantha Bertram. He'd previously noticed Fiona was given to displaying considerable cleavage which could be construed in a conservative office environment as being inappropriate: now, more than just her cleavage was on display as she stood, the straps of her dress pulled down and her breasts fully exposed. She was positioned by the far wall, facing the door, and those fully exposed breasts and erect nipples were pointing directly at Robert: he couldn't help but notice their pertness given the woman's age.

Samantha was in front of her, bent forwards with her torso splayed on the table and her buttocks raised pointing towards Fiona. She was naked. She looked at Robert with an expression that was a combination of alarm and salaciousness: her face and neck were flushed, and so it appeared were her buttocks.

Robert started as he attempted to process the scene, sputtered wordlessly, and began to back away.

Dexter eyed Robert with a firm expression. "Sit!" she commanded, pointing to a chair to Robert's right which was pushed back against the wall.

Ashton couldn't bring himself to speak, and instead, silently, did as he was bid. Sitting side-on to the table, he could now see both women in full view.

Bertram had a fuller figure, but her curves were in all the right places, and her glowing buttocks quivered as Dexter cracked an open palm against them with a whipcracking slap. Samantha let out a small gasp which combined an equal measure of pleasure and pain. Robert winced as Dexter laid another three equally sharp blows to the younger woman's posterior, and she bit her lip to stifle her voice.

Fiona stopped and stepped back, placing her hands on her hips. Her chest was heaving with the exertion and a light film of perspiration made the skin on her naked torso shine under the bright artificial light. Then she moved forward, and leaned over Samantha, her breasts pressing into her back, and she reached down to place a hand under her partner's arse and began to massage her cunt, at first slowly, but soon building to a rapid, almost violent, pace. Samantha squeaked breathlessly as orgasms wracked her body and she shuddered, arching her back and lifting herself up from her prone position on the table.

Then, carefully but with a certain amount of force, Fiona wrapped a fist of Samantha's hair and slowly pulled her upwards, guiding her into a standing position before turning her around and pushing her back so she was seated on the table. The dominatrix first planted the younger woman's face between her own breasts and held it there, hard, until she could barely breathe. She then began to massage Samantha's immense breasts, becoming increasingly forceful until she was kneeding the mounds in big, deep circular motions, before she moved her face toward them and began licking, nipping and nibbling at her protruding nipples. All the while, she worked her fingers in and out of Samantha's dripping snatch. Samantha's breath came in juddering gasps, and she bit her finger to restrain her cries.

Robert sat, silent, trembling. This was by far the most bizarre and awkward scene he had witnessed in an office in his entire career, and while he had not viewed either women in a sexual light previously, it was impossible for him to feel anything other than aroused now. He watched on, bewildered as Fiona buried her face in Samantha's quim, lapping vigorously between her parted lips. Her pubic hair was slick with juice and saliva, and the blush that ruddied her face and neck now extended down over her bouncing orbs as she orgasmed hard.

At this, Dexter stopped and stood upright, before taking a step back. She pointed wordlessly at the floor by her feet. At this gesture, Bertram slipped down from the table and knelt before her mistress, who raised the knee-length skirt of her dress to reveal her shaven snatch. Fiona simply gave a look, and Samantha began to lick away at her labia, meekly working her tongue into the hole. Exalted, Dexter grabbed her hair and pulled her face hard into her pubis, grinding hard and clenching her teeth as she rode the waves of ecstasy. Robert couldn't help but watch the way Samantha's huge tits swung as she thrust her face into the dark orifice.

Robert felt dizzy and nervous as Fiona released Samantha and walked toward him. He had known and experienced his share of women, but Dexter's aggressive sexual appetite unnerved him. He had all but forgotten the teleconference as she rubbed a hand over his crotch, gently squeezing his hard-on through his trousers. His cock throbbed as she slowly but deftly unzipped his fly, leaning towards his and brushing his face lightly with her nipples. He fought the instinct to lick them, aware that he had no wish to be an active participant in this outlandish sex act.

Retail Island

Fiona popped his pulsating penis out of his fly and with remarkable gentleness, massaged the length of his shaft. Robert found himself in a fugue-like state, immobile and mute. She quickened the pace and increased the roughness of her handling, but not so much so as to inflict pain. Then, just as Robert was on the brink of orgasm, she stopped. She straightened her skirt and pulled the straps of her dress, reholstering her breasts. Behind her, Samantha was hurriedly pulling on her dress. In moments, and without a word, they marched briskly and business-like from the room, leaving Robert alone with his erection and a cluster of confused thoughts.

Retail Island

Part 2: Nobody wants to be here, and nobody wants to leave

Fay had been right. The following Saturday, the immense Primark store, that had been under wraps and swarming with construction workers and fitters when Robert had landed at the retail park, opened its doors to the public. The event was distinguished by queues not only at the checkouts, but in the aisles, on the forecourt, and halfway around the perimeter walkways, as eager shoppers crowded and jostled to gain entry to the vast warehouse packed with sweatshop-manufactured clothing. Queues also began to build in the car parks as shoppers arrived in droves.

Long before midday, the retail park's parking spaces were all occupied, as were those of the neighbouring Asda and Sainsbury's superstores, and many had simply abandoned their vehicles on the access roads, pavements, and verges in and around the development. Robert had only ventured out to WH Smith to purchase a magazine and newspaper in order to sequester himself away in his hotel room for a day of rest, but even this brief excursion swiftly evolved into a major operation as he was forced to navigate by a wildly circuitous route and battle his way through the crowd which had spilled out to occupy a large area of the park.

"Hey!" a large woman in grey sweatpants and a voluminous T-shirt bearing the slogan 'Whatchoo Lookin at.... Bitch?' barked as Robert tried to inch his way through a conglomeration of milling shoppers. He glanced up automatically. She seemed to be staring straight at him, but assuming she must have been trying to get the attention of someone behind him, Robert glanced over his shoulder. "Yeah, you," she said gruffly. "Where d'you fink you're goin'?"

"I'm sorry?" Robert blinked.

"Yer will be," she growled in response. "We been 'ere fuckin' ages waitin' t'gerrin, so instead o' pushin' frough y'need t'wait yer turn."

"Oh, right, I see," Robert said. "In there?" he pointed toward Primark.

"Yeh. We was 'ere first."

"Of course. I was just trying to get through to get to WS Smith, I'm not going in there, so..."

"Yeah, fuckin' right. I've 'eard all kinds of excuses to push frough. Meetin' a family member. Lost kids. Member o' staff. One guy even said 'ee were a fuckin' medic attendin' a 'mergency 'cause someone'd passed out. As if! Cheeky fucker. So y'reckon I'm gunna buy that you wanna go to Smiffs?"

"But I *do*," Robert protested.

"Yeah, fuck off out of it," the woman snarled, bearing her teeth and revealing numerous gaps amid yellowed, nicotine-stained, pegs.

A burly man wearing similar attire – an England football shirt stretched over his gut – tattoos and shaven head, stepped up, bristling. "You 'eard the lady. Get the fuck out, you cunt."

Robert wasn't so sure about the status of his antagonist as a lady, but didn't have time to dwell on that as the thug stepped forward and shoved him hard in the chest. Robert stumbled back and was just able to keep his footing, but knocked into a woman who was trying to steer a pushchair through the dense forest of bodies.

"Excuse me!" she shouted coarsely in a 40-a-day voice.

"I'm sorry."

"So you should be!" she snapped. "You need to look where you're bloody going!"

Robert tried to explain, but had merely stammered a few unintelligible syllables before another man stepped up beside the woman and began berating him for being a 'posho cunt'. Before he knew what was happening, Robert found himself knocked to the ground, and a tempest of fists and trainer-toed feet rained blows about his body. He curled himself tightly into a ball, and before long, following a foot to the skull, lost consciousness. The sound of the crowd diminished as everything faded to black.

****

Robert came to in a fog of white light. His eyes swam and his body ached, throbbed, pulsated. More than that, it crackled and exploded with pain. So much pain: it was impossible to determine the individual sources of the separate pains which formed a cumulative, full-body agony. It hurt to open his eyes; it hurt to breathe. It hurt simply to *be*. Given the searing pain which inhaling precipitated, he resisted the urge to speak and simply lay as still as possible, deducing by moving his eyes, and, to a lesser extent, his wooden neck, that he was in hospital. His head was muzzy and felt as if it was full of wet cotton wool, but he could recall fragmented images of the crowd swarming him after a vulgar woman led the assault. Thus far, the narrative sequence seemed corollary, although he couldn't recall how the sequence began. There was a gap, a leap from walking around the retail park to effectively being lynched. But there was enough floating in his cerebellum to forge an adequately coherent sequence of events for Robert to piece together an acceptably functional linear narrative which directed him to his present state without the need to resort to dialogical cliché.

He wasn't sure how long he had lain in this state of semi-delirium before a nurse approached him, although he would later learn that the nurses arrival at his bedside had been quickened significantly by one of his colleagues.

"Robert? Can you hear me?" the nurse asked as she slowly swam into focus.

Robert nodded slowly, his head feeling like a leaden weight. "I can see you too."

"Good, good. Do you know why you're here?" The nurse was large, a generous 18-22, with straw-yellow hair that looked brittle. Her pudgy features were still hazy and indistinct around the edges.

Robert nodded again with a pained wince. "Yes. A large, aggressive woman lead the attack. I was near the new Primark."

"You should probably save the detail for the police. I'm pleased to say your brain function seems normal, and you don't even appear to have sustained any concussion. In fact, you're a borderline miracle!"

Ashton must have drifted back into unconsciousness shortly after, and for how long he was uncertain, but dark hair was the next swampy point of focus which registered with Robert shortly after. He blinked repeatedly, trying to clear his foggy eyes, but to no avail.

"I came as soon as I could," a soothing local voice said.

It took for a moment to register with Robert that the voice belonged to Fay.

"How did you find me?" Robert asked, confused.

"Don't worry about that right now," Fay said. "Let's concentrate on getting you home – or at least, back to the hotel and back to work."

"Part of me thinks that this is all part of the work," Robert grimaced as he shunted himself up.

"I think you're probably right," the brunette replied, her features coming into sharper focus as Robert blinked a few more times.

She looked straight at him, intent, and he noticed the blueness of her eyes. He felt a flicker of something, but dismissed it as being some kind of post-traumatic reaction.

"I'm usually right," he replied, pushing the flicker away as best he could.

It took another six-and-a-half hours before Robert was discharged, but Fay patiently stayed with him for the duration, chatting amiably about anything and everything, but stubbornly avoiding the topic of work in a perceived public setting.

"You're unnerving me a little with your paranoia," Robert told her at one point during the interminable wait.

"You can't be too careful," she replied simply, and Robert knew to let it drop.

****

Robert was fortunate to have an understanding wife in Jude – at least he assumed and trusted she was understanding, and he didn't anxietise over her activities or whereabouts during his absence. Sitting on the sofa in Fay's flat, nursing a glass of red wine, his ribs tender and aching, and with sharp pain shooting around his torso each time he inhaled, Robert was acutely aware that the situation was loaded with awkward and uncomfortable potentialities, despite its innocence. Faye's ex-husband was working away, and her children were staying with her parents for a few days over the holidays, he learned on arrival at her home after a short drive in her small car. She was, Robert had noted, chatty, and free with information about the day-to-day aspects of her life, if not her deeper concerns. The way she looked at him, and sometimes in the way she spoke, Robert couldn't help but feel a certain flirtatiousness, but he dismissed this as simply her demeanour rather than something directed a him specifically. Nevertheless, he had warmed to her, and was convinced if nothing else of her sincerity.

Robert was unable to resist the compulsion to return to a previous topic. "You do seem quite paranoid," he said gently as she poured each of them a second glass of wine.

"I am," she replied plainly. "It's the job." She hesitated. "Ok, it's me as well. I *am* paranoid. I get jumpy about the smallest thing, and that's just how I am. I'm a bit OCD, too. You probably don't need to know all this. But there's something about you I just sense I can trust. And actually, I suppose you need to know that I don't trust people often because I'm going to trust you with this, and I don't want you to think I'm just some loose-tongued gossip who spills company secrets all over the place. You'll probably think I'm nuts anyway."

Robert could tell she was becoming agitated, and despite his aversion to physical contact, put a hand on her arm in an attempt to calm her down. "It's ok," he said in his most measured tone.

She stopped abruptly and caught her breath. "Sorry," she said.

"Don't be," Robert replied evenly.

"Ok. Look, this is hard," she said, further building her preamble.

"It's ok. Take your time."

"I was on projects. The way the company operates, as you probably know now, is on a need-to-know basis. So what they do is carve up projects into segments, so no-one knows everything. Or sometimes anything, or at least anything useful."

"I'd noticed. This is exactly how Project Mushroom is being operated. On the one hand, I get it, but on the other, it's frustrating and it makes me suspicious. And also acutely aware of the connotations of the project's name: it's the cliché of being kept in the dark and fed on shit."

"I think there are other levels to Project Mushroom," Fay intimated. She spoke quietly and picked at her lip.

"What have they done to you?" asked Robert, squinting and curious.

"Nothing specific," Fay replied, looking pained.

Robert felt his brow furrow with concern: he couldn't help it. It was clear to him that Fay was no manipulator.

"Ok…" he offered encouragingly.

"Ok, on previous projects it was clear that Medico had questionable ethics. In particular – actually, two things. The first is that they don't seem to be as concerned with creating drugs to cure people or make them feel better, as mess them up. This will probably sound crazy, but it's like they want to make people ill."

"That doesn't sound crazy," Robert said gently but firmly. "Listen, I got shut down, hard, when I questioned the purpose of Project Mushroom. But the fact is that the drug or whatever it is they're working on is an airborne pro-psychotic, designed to affect behavioural patterns in certain places at given times. The launch date for the testing was on Saturday. In other words, I think the fact I got lynched was actually part of the initial testing. They're looking to create a drug they can pump into the air to determine behaviours. Although why they'd want to steer violent behaviour is beyond me. Perhaps that was a flaw in the makeup and they're looking at creating a more balanced form of mind control. Even so..."

"I worry that's only the tip of the iceberg," Fay confided, casting her eyes downwards. "Manipulation of behaviour seems to be an overarching theme."

Robert studied her solemn face for a moment; he contemplated her even teeth and smooth skin, and began to wonder if this, or she, wasn't some kind of experiment in itself. He fought a sudden compulsion to grab her hand and place himself on a limb for her. He dismissed this as an aftereffect of the attack, and immediately dismissed and compartmentalised it as some misaligned manifestation of Nightingale syndrome, but it didn't sit any more comfortably than the prospect of airborne substances circulating to effect mind control. If any of this were true, he was witnessing, and involved in, the most comprehensive and unethical mind-control experiment since MK Ultra. Robert was a clinical, rational, and balanced individual, and yet he was growing increasingly suspicious. As such, while he didn't want any of it to be true, he couldn't help feeling that perhaps it was.

"I've not been here long, but I've already seen plenty of strange behaviours in the office," he said after a time. "Plenty of *really* strange behaviours," he added, with emphasis. He didn't feel able to bring himself to say it.

"No shit," Fay shot back bluntly. "You're talking about the way people seem to get it on at random? Or the other weird shit?"

"Well, now you put I like that... yes." Robert was taken aback, but kept his shock well under wraps.

"I suspected as much,"

"Really?"

"It's rife."

"Have you...?"

"No. I've always been resistant."

"How have you managed that?"

"I'm not sure. Some genetic defect or something, probably. I worry that they'll pursue me harder at some point in an attempt to unravel why I'm not susceptible and that they're just biding their time."

"So why don't you get out?"

"I'm torn. I want to see what happens. And I've got bills to pay."

Sharing a momentary anxiety, they held one another's gaze for a full minute, and then wordlessly, they embraced. Their lips locked for a moment, and they spiralled into darkness as they were each immersed in it. Coming up for air, they stared into one another's eyes again. Robert resisted the urge to declare his love to her and Fay already had flushed cheeks.

"This is exactly what they want," said Fay.

"So, what do *we* want?"

"To get the project together, and to talk openly. And in the meantime, play along with them so they think they've got us under control." She gave a conspiratorial smile.

"Are you sure you're not susceptible?"

"Positive."

****

Robert accepted Fay's invitation to stay the night, opting to take the spare room. Despite their earlier moment of intimacy, it felt wrong to progress further under the circumstances. Robert had recounted his experience on Friday, and they had discussed at length the increasing prickliness they felt around the notion of sexual encounters amid the orgiastic atmosphere of the Medico office. Fay detailed the long, slow decline in her marriage which ultimately led to divorce, and how she had gradually become increasingly prone to stress and anxiety after she began her career at Medico shortly after the separation.

"Ever considered that the anxiety was connected to Medico, rather than the separation and divorce?" Robert asked as Fay poured them each another glass of wine. They were now halfway down the third bottle.

"No," Fay confessed. "But now you mention it...." She trailed off.

They had been listening to the local radio, with news updates reporting on how there had been a number of incidents including reports of fights and damage at Ebor Park on the opening of the new Primark store. It seemed Robert had not been the sole victim of abuse and physical violence as shoppers had clamoured for goods.

"This is madness." Robert murmured. "Could you go for the national TV news for a moment?"

Fay nodded and turned on the television. Sure enough, the events at Ebor Park had made the national news. The footage was sparse, culled from shaky mobile phone material with poor audio quality, but showed people pushing and shoving in crowds, accompanied by much angry shouting. The newscaster reported that more than a dozen people had been hospitalised as a result of the ructions, one of whom was flagged as critical.

Fay gaped open-mouthed. "Shit," she mumbled, her brow furrowing.

Robert observed with detachment that concern suited her, and rendered her pale features somehow all the more attractive. The furrows on her forehead mapped the contours of her anxiety, and drew in clear relief the geographical planes of her psyche. It was, he reflected, the depth of empathy which subconsciously sculpted her features, and the anguish glowed in her tired eyes which fitted her so comfortably.

"We need to get back to the retail park," Robert said resolutely.

"But you could have been really badly hurt," Fay protested.

"This isn't about my personal safety," Robert said. "There's research to be done, for the greater good."

"Do you think this could escalate?" Fay's expression of concern was building toward panic.

"I believe that's actually the intention," Robert affirmed. "And I need to be there to witness and report it."

"But not tonight," Fay said, firmly, pouring another glass of wine.

****

Retail Island

Fay insisted Robert had a lie-in after his ordeal, and as he ate the breakfast she had prepared him – a simple but generous repast of copious hot drinks and endless slices of hot buttered toast – he contemplated his next move. He wasn't entirely clear of his own motives, and even less so of his operational instructions with regard to Project Mushroom. However, he was torn between the notion that the wheels were rapidly coming off the cart that was the project, and the opinion that the project was gaining the momentum it sought but wasn't fully equipped for. Either way, none of this had been in his briefings, and Robert felt at this juncture that he was cut adrift and existed in a no-man's land located between the domains of ambivalence and antagonism in relation to the project. At this moment in time, the non-disclosure agreement was less than worthless, given that, even now, Robert effectively knew less than nothing, and moreover, he felt a greater duty to society than to Medico or himself if the company's experiments and events at Ebor Park took the turn they seemingly threatened to.

Fay pointed out that as it was Sunday, and the shops didn't open till 11am, there was little point in hurrying to the retail park, and the Medico office would be running on a skeletal staff of IT workers. There would, therefore, she reasoned, be no point on crashing the office.

"It pains me to say that you're right," Robert said as he sipped the coffee Fay had made him. She didn't drink coffee herself, instead consuming large quantities of strong, sugary tea, but she made a decent coffee.

"I'm always right," she replied with a flirtatious smile, shot from beneath her fringe.

Robert rolled his eyes and smiled back at her. Despite the gravity of the situation, which they both clearly grasped, there was a light-hearted thread to their exchanges which was hard to deny, and which kept Robert from expending a surfeit of time and energy exploring darker mental avenues.

****

Checking the local news that Sunday morning, Robert and Fay learned jointly of the continued escalation of events at Ebor Park, which had seen a number of shoppers refusing to leave the shopping complex on Saturday night.

Curiously, the story had completely disappeared from the BBC and Sky websites, and all other national and international news outlets.

"So where're you going first?" Fay asked.

"I'm still not sure of the benefit of the office," Robert replied, sipping his coffee and thinking how strangely comfortable the scenario felt: eating breakfast with Fay, he felt more like he was in a married relationship than dining with a woman he barely knew and felt a vague sexual attraction to. As for that sexual attraction, Robert struggled to place it as he subconsciously assessed the contours of her face and her overall geometry: she was trim, attractive, but understated. He found that understatedness a source of attraction in itself. But this was simply one further layer in the complexity of their undefined relationship.

"So, where? Primark? You could end up taking another battering if you try wandering in there..." She sounded irritated, but her annoyance masked an unintended degree of concern.

"Possibly," Robert mused. "The retail park is the place I think we'll get a better sense of the manifestations of the experiment, at least in terms of results. I don't know where the fuck to start with

Medico. It feels so shambolic and fragmented, organisationally, but a part of me wonders if this isn't strategic and part of the willful obfuscation of its actual motivations and practices."

"Is Jack Barham worth leaning on, do you think?" Fay asked.

"Hard to say," Robert pondered. "Do *you* think?"

"Part of me is trying not to think. But perhaps. Vague and bombastic as he seems, I think he knows more than he's letting on, and perhaps actually has more steer than is apparent."

"Good to know," Robert nodded. "So now we need to figure out how to break him down a bit."

"We need to break him down as hard as you were yesterday," Fay said sarcastically, but with a smile.

Robert started to laugh but the pain in his damaged ribs halted his amusement abruptly. In the bathroom mirror, he had already observed that his face was a mottled patchwork of contusions, and he figured his torso and much of the rest of his body would begin to bloom an array of yellows greens, purples, blues, and blacks over the coming hours and days. His body felt a little stiff and his brain a bit foggy, but his resolve was strong enough to keep him sharp enough for the task at hand.

Driving toward the complex in Fay's Aygo as the clock crept toward 1pm, they debated yet again their first port of call: the Medico office, or the retail park itself.

"I really do have my reservations about Jack," Robert said. It felt good to be able to speak freely with Fay, although he did find himself flinching occasionally over just how much he had so readily divulged to her.

"Personally, I think he's dangerous," Fay replied, without hesitation.

"Dangerous how?" Robert quizzed.

"Look, he's powerful," Fay said evenly. "He's headed a lot of projects. And a lot of people have disappeared from those projects."

"Disappeared?"

"Yes. I don't have any more detail. They've been seconded to projects. They've disappeared. Some officially, as in reported missing and never found, some simply just never heard from or mentioned again. The end."

"I don't believe that's the end."

"Me neither, and that's partly why we're here."

Retail Island

They continued to discuss various strategic approaches as Fay drove them towards Ebor Park. As they drew within half a mile, they joined a large queue of traffic. Searching for information on the Internet, Robert found nothing of real note, other than the previous day's news about the outbreaks of violence and the growing number of shoppers refusing to leave the park. Again, he mused over the various uses of 'park', from the verb to park one's vehicle via the play park and the deer park to the unnatural concrete desert of the retail park. Robert much preferred the 'large public garden or area of land used for recreation' to the 'area devoted to a specified purpose' which incorporated the industrial or retail park, and sitting in near-stationary traffic he felt his agitation rising once more.

Fay flipped on the radio and turned to the local radio station. The first fifteen minutes was given to 'classic' tracks from the 1970s and 1980s and inane babble about a local charity fête and the weather, but finally it arrived at a segment about the unprecedented reaction to the opening of the new clothing store at Ebor Park. They warned of congestion as shoppers flocked to the retail centre, but gave no detail beyond that. It was as if the riots and the violence weren't happening. It took them an hour to travel the last quarter of a mile and the car park was completely full, to the extent that they had to drive round for over forty minutes to find a space on a verge outside the perimeter of the retail park. On a number of occasions, as they had initially tried to find a space in the car park, other had drivers lurched aggressively into spaces, or otherwise blocked their access. The atmosphere was tense and ugly, and they witnessed a number of fights breaking out as shoppers battled over parking spaces. Mostly, these consisted of exchanges of verbal abuse accompanied by the occasional ill-directed blow, but they were sickened to see a young family in sportswear drag a pensioner in a waxed Barbour jacket from his Citroën C1. They proceeded to kick, punch and spit on him for having allegedly nipped into the spot they had been clearly about to move into.

Pulling her little car quietly and unnoticed into the improvised parking space beyond the peripheries of the immense expanse of tarmac, Fay let out a quiet sigh of relief: the experience had clearly distressed her.

Retail Island

"You really want to go out there, and into *that?*" she asked.

"I have to," Robert replied resolutely.

****

The atmosphere around the shops was electric and increasingly ugly as shoppers jostled one another to join the disorderly assemblage – it was no longer a queue – outside Primark. Robert elected to call into a handful of other retailers to begin with, and was genuinely amazed by just how empty they were. First, he casually rifled the clothing rails of H&M, before selecting a pair of dark plastic sunglasses in the sale section with a view to covering his shiner. It felt strange shopping for clothes with Fay shadowing him: Jude had never been the kind of wife with whom he had gone clothed shopping, and while she generally detested his choice of patterned shirts, she had proven herself less than keen to accompany him to assist with the selection of alternatives.

Robert had not had even so much as text-message contact with Jude since Friday night, before the incident which had seen him hospitalized. He gave this fact considerable thought before resolving to call her that evening. He felt that they had become increasingly distant in recent months, and figured he ought to make at least some effort, even it was but once every eight weeks they spent time enough together for a meal.

He strolled up to the counter where the two checkout staff stood leaning boredly against the counter. The svelte blonde who leaped forward to serve him didn't need to force her smile: she looked genuinely pleased to have something to do, even if it was only to sell a man in his late thirties a pair of cheap sunglasses.

"It seems pretty dead in here," Ashton remarked as he placed the shades on the counter. "Where is everyone?"

The blonde looked a little uncomfortable and cast an eye through her sweeping fringe. "Out there, I think," she replied in a husky voice. "Have you seen the queue for Primark?"

"I have, yes. It's not so much a queue as a riotous frenzy."

"Yes, everyone's gone mad for it, and it seems to be the only shop they come for."

"It's mental," interjected the chubby redhead who had been standing, motionless, at her till.

"Everyone's just turned up to go there, like it's the first Primark on the planet."

The blonde turned to her, a smile spreading on her sallow face. "Yeah, that's just it. It's like they've never seen cheap clothes," she said, shaking her head.

"But why?" asked Robert, half bewildered, despite his *a priori* knowledge.

The blonde shrugged her slender shoulders, from which a khaki cardigan hung limply, as uninspired as her face and body language. "Dunno," she said, blandly. "It's actually like they've been literally brainwashed."

Robert paid and bade the bored staff at the clothing store farewell.

****

Stepping out, Robert cast his eye toward the ruckus that continued to build as more and more clamoured toward the doors of Primark. Something subconscious made him cast his eyes upward, and he noticed a figure on the roof of the retail unit. It took a moment for him to cognise that the figure was none other than Jack Barham. He was positioned near the ledge, a camera trained on the increasingly angry-looking mob. Robert was unable to make out his expression at such distance, but his posture was one of imposing dominance.

Robert felt his phone vibrate. It was a message from Fay, over on the other side of the retail park, reporting the outbreak of a number of fights in and around Asda as customers were attempting to shoplift large quantities of food, as well as expensive electricals and other high-value goods, including large-screen televisions, laptops, Dysons, not to mention PlayStation games, Blu-ray discs, perfume, and shoes, and household items. Significantly, she'd spotted Tom Grindstaff and Steve Thompson on the peripheries, their phones out, and seemingly taking photographs and shooting other footage of the events as they unraveled.

"The fuck..?" The words slipped from Ashton's mouth under his breath as an incredulous whisper. It wasn't proof *per se*, but surely this provided the link between Medico and the strangely turning events that he needed to take things further. But further where? The trouble with whistleblowing on conspiracies involving high-funded corporations with government connections is that it's invariably the integrity – and sanity – of the whistle-blower which is called into question long before that of the company, or the government. Robert had always been suspicious of the conclusion of suicide surrounding the death of Dr David Kelly in the wake of the September Dossier in 2003.

A paranoia gripped Robert now as he contemplated any reports submitted in relation to the operations at Medico. Between fleeting visions of the rampant sex acts he had witnessed during his brief stint at Medico, which included flashbacks of Jack Barham's glistening penis as he ejaculated long spurts of jissom over the immense globular orbs of the anonymous girl in the toilets, and his own first-hand experience of wild antics between Fiona Dexter and Samantha Bertram, which had locked a mental polaroid of Samantha's immense nipples in his mind, a fog of confusion coupled with a throb in his groin rendered his thought process unreliable. Of this, he was convinced. His rational side reminded him that no-one other than Fay knew the full details of what he had witnessed, and he could trust her. Or could he? Doubt reeled in his increasingly crowded mind, and he felt his chest tighten and his breath quicken.

He had to speak to Barham, but first he needed to speak with Fay, and to get his head clear. Looking out over the increasingly raucous crowd, Robert felt that he needed to first focus, and to break from the crowd. Agitation rising, he felt dizzy and stumbled onwards through the crowds toward the Asda ruckus.

****

Retail Island

Robert waded his way through the crowd, the majority of whom were lumbering through the car park toward the insane mob clamouring outside Primark – at least thirty rows deep and all pressing together, shouting and jostling against the security guards now installed in front of the shop's doors. The burly men in uniforms of T-Shirts and combat trousers had their work cut out as the swelling numbers pushed to gain entrance to the store.

"Shithead, I need to get my daughter some fucking clothes," a woman was screaming at one of the security guards. He stood impassively, telling her there was nothing he could do.

Another security guard, with a shaven head, and who must have stood at least six and a half feet in height and weighed twenty stone, was holding a scrawny man with a limp moustache at arm's length and repeating that he must wait this turn. "But I've been waiting hours," the man protested whinily, "I've been sitting in the car-park overnight."

"Not my problem, mate," the guard shot back gruffly. "So have half the folks here."

Robert noticed one of the security guards with his trousers pulled down to his knees and a woman in front of him with her hands and forearms around his thick, muscular, rugby-player thighs as she gobbled hard on his stubby, circumcised penis. Her tongue lashed against the engorged head and he closed his eyes as he shot his hot load across her face. He jerked his head toward the door. The woman, a blonde in her mid-twenties, smiled as she wiped the gunk from her eyes and made her way into the store.

Shocked by the desperation, Robert spotted another familiar figure some way to his left: it was the thick-set form of Phil Thompson, and he was was engrossed in filming the various altercations and exchanges, documenting the clamorous hubbub as it swelled to ever greater proportions. A grin was on his face as his lens followed the woman who had administered the fellatio. Robert felt his pulse quicken and his muscles tense a little at the sight. As he battled his way towards Asda and Fay, mindful not to knock anyone or make eye contact so as to avoid any potential confrontation, he observed myriad scuffles and altercations. Most were minor, but he felt a wave or nausea course through his body at the sight of a young woman lying prone on the ground, her clothes torn, and with gouts of blood pouring from a gash in her bruised head. She was missing a trainer and her expression was haunted and vacant-looking. It was clear she'd taken quite a mauling, but Robert had no time to stop and help her as another outbreak of violence erupted just feet away. This time, three women and a young male were laying into a man who appeared to be in his thirties, battering him with full bags of shopping, fists, and feet. One of the women, sporting a tight denim mini-dress, was clutching a high-heeled shoe in one hand, which she was using to land blows to the man's head and torso.

"Stop it! Stop it, please," a woman pleaded, her face streaming tears. "Leave him alone."

"Do you want some too?" one of the women asked, landing a sharp slap to the crying woman's ear.

"Has anyone called the emergency services?" Robert asked, turning to a family of onlookers who were standing, motionless and vacant-looking.

"Yes," replied a dark-haired man in a suit, "But they can't get through because of the traffic. They're stuck about a mile away."

Robert's phone vibrated again, with another message from Fay urging him to hurry as things had taken another yet more violent turn by Asda. He was torn, as the fracas before him was rapidly escalating, with bystanders wading in on both sides, strangers exchanging blows in support of the beleaguered couple and joining the gang who were attacking them. It still wasn't clear what the fight was about or who had provoked it, but the scene was growing increasingly ugly, and as Robert slipped away, it had escalated to a brawl with maybe twenty or more participants flailing fists and feet, pulling hair and clawing blindly.

****

By the Asda store front, Robert discovered similar scenes, only on an even wider and more brutal scale. This came as a surprise, despite all that he had already witnessed in recent days. Outside, a swelling crowd was becoming increasingly agitated and those at the front were hammering and kicking at the doors. It took Robert a moment to get enough of a view to see that several of the doors had been barricaded from the inside. He spotted Fay standing on the peripheries of the mob, looking anxious, and he felt his own anxiety rising higher from the pit of his stomach as he broke into a nervous perspiration.

He made his way toward her, again mindful not to nudge or make eye contact with anyone.

"What's going on?" he asked, even though he realised she wouldn't know any more than he had already seen for himself.

"As far as I can tell, the shoppers inside have decided they don't want anyone else to go in, and they don't want to come out," she said. "From overhearing some of the conversations on phones and the security radios, they've tampered with the automatic doors somehow so they won't open, and they're physically barricading themselves in with display units and whatever else they can get their hands on."

"Given that no-one seems particularly eager to go home, I'm guessing the people in the supermarket want to protect the food supplies for themselves. And I think the number of Medico staff in the vicinity documenting events confirms my initial theory that they're engineering some kind of disruptive social behaviours. What I don't know is whether this was the desired effect, or if things are running out of control."

"Given my experience of Medico," Fay said grimly, "it's purely experimental at this stage, so nothing is considered out of control."

"But the way things are heating up, people are going to die," Robert said, panic rising.

"Isn't that always the case with medical trials?" asked Fay with a certain resignation.

"Maybe so," Robert conceded, "but this is a whole new level of insanity we're seeing here. We need to get to Jack Barham to see if he can do something to put a stop to this before it escalates beyond a mere riot situation into all-out war."

"I don't know if he's got that kind of power," Fay said, shaking her head.

"He's the most senior person on the project at the office and who we have a direct line to," Robert replied, "which means he's the best chance we've got. Besides, he's definitely calling some of the shots, even if only the ones that operate on a local level."

Robert looked to see if he could still see Barham on the roof of Primark, but he was unable to get a clear view over the distance. He did, however, spot a face he recognised nearby: it belonged to Vicky Hoyle, who had accompanied Jack to meet him on his first day. Her jaw was clenched firm with concentration, but there was a glint in her eye which corresponded with the self-satisfied smile that kinked her lips. As he made his way toward her, the crowd's attention was diverted by the rumble of rotors growing increasingly near. Collectively, heads lifted toward the sky, although many ignored the rising volume from above as they continued to focus on jostling, shoving, and shouting, angry expressions fixed on their faces. A handful of people cheered as they recognised the air ambulance, although Robert already knew there were more injured people lying in the battlefield that the expanse of tarmac had become than a single helicopter could ever accommodate. Nevertheless, he felt a flicker of optimism at the thought that this may just be the first of the emergency services to find its way over the traffic jam – local news on the Internet now suggested tailbacks trailed for some two miles in all directions out from Ebor Park. Perhaps sanity and order could be restored without the need for Medico to scale back their operations and the project could be shelved.

The rush of air from the blades forced many to move away from the space the helicopter's pilot was now attempting to lower it down to, and as the door at the side of the vehicle opened, one of the medics appeared and began to gesticulate for those below to clear the area. As the bodies began to mill out of the way, a beer-bellied skinhead charged through the crowd and positioned himself directly beneath the chopper's hulk, waving his fists and yelling profanities at the craft's undercarriage. He was soon joined by a motley array of other objectors, including a number of overweight men in sweat pants and T-shirts, and women in bone-tight stonewashed jeans and vest tops, who began loudly and vociferously protesting the helicopter's presence.

"Fuck off!" one of the men shouted, barely audible above the roar of the updraft. "We don't need you here! Just fucking leave us alone!"

"Yeah, leave us alone!" the others jeered in a football terrace chorus.

The helicopter continued to hover and the medic looked perturbed by the turn of events, clearly uncertain as to how to react.

Just then, an object sailed into the frame and crashed through one of the front windows of the helicopter. Robert turned to observe a man hurl a brick, pulled from the border of the nearest island tree, at the aircraft, and this also smashed through the same front window. The pilot ducked and only just avoided the missile as it flew into the cockpit. But before long, a cluster of protestors had gathered near the sapling and were hurling uprooted masonry at the vehicle. As missiles rained in through the windshields, the pilot began to lose his focus, his attention divided between maintaining the helicopter's position above the car park and avoiding the objects exploding through the windows. Perhaps inevitably, one caught him square in the temple, knocking him unconscious. Within seconds, the air ambulance crashed to the ground, crushing a number of the marauders rampaging below, as well as some innocent bystanders unable to get out of the way. In an instant, and angry mob surged aboard the broken vehicle and dragged the crew out onto the car park, punching, kicking and swearing. They battered them with handles from shopping trolleys, lengths of railings uprooted from outside shops and more pieces of brick torn from the tree borders. Within minutes, all of the helicopter's crew lay, broken, bleeding, and dead on the tarmac.

****

Retail Island

There were shrieks and screams all around, but Robert noticed that Vicky Hoyle remained steady and impassive, continuing to capture events as they happened on her company iPhone. Unlike many others, she made no effort to aid either the trampled medical team or those wounded by the crashing helicopter crash-landed. The bodies which lay strewn on the hard, black ground were soon forgotten by the seething masses trying to press their way into Primark and Asda, the entrances to the latter of which were now fully barricaded.

"Vicky," Robert gasped having pressed his way through to the tall, slender brunette in a slim-fitting jacket and pinstripe pencil-skirt.

She turned to him with a mixture of confusion and fury which filled him with perplexity. "What?" she snapped.

Robert wasn't sure if she recognised him. "This..." Robert began hesitantly, shrugging and lifting his arms limply.

"Robert, isn't it?" she quizzed, her eyes boring into him.

"Yes," Ashton affirmed, anxiously.

"Why are you here?" Hoyle asked with a hard edge to her tone.

"To be honest, I don't really know, but I was hired by Medico to work on Project Mushroom," Robert said. "And I think we need to talk," he added.

Vicky's expression softened a little but retained an air of questioning. Robert reflected that if she didn't portray such a hard exterior, with her dark hair scraped back and her mouth pinched – and judging by the puckering of her lips she was, or at least had been for some time, a heavy smoker – she may have been attractive, at least five or ten years ago. "Do you?" she asked, her intonation a combination of authoritarian brittleness and surprise.

Robert nodded gently, a technique he had learned on a number of counselling courses. "Yes," he affirmed, "I believe we do."

Disarmed by Ashton's tranquility in a surging maelstrom of escalating violence, Hoyle acquiesced. "At the office?"

"That would be ideal, but I don't see a way we could possibly escape. I heard there are blockades on both the north and east entrances, which are the ways to the Medico office."

"There are. They've jammed the exits with blockades of cars. Those who are here aren't leaving, and they're not going to let anyone else in, however much they want in. But do you know the tunnel?" she asked.

"No?" Robert adopted the Australian inflection, the note rising up to denote a question.

"I thought all Project Mushroom operatives were supposed to have been made aware of the tunnel," she said, her voice a mixture of sympathy and irritation. "Who was your briefing operative?"

"Jack Barham," Robert replied evenly, factually, and without malice. The fact was that while Robert increasingly considered Barham to be a dangerous individual, in possession of an excessive and irresponsible degree of power, none of his interaction with Jack had given any real foundation for this opinion, and Robert always liked to give the benefit of the doubt to even the shiftiest of customers.

Unexpectedly, Vicky rolled her eyes. "Look, there's a manhole cover over past Primark, near the cash point to the immediate left of the Boots unit," she said, leaning close so her voice could be heard over the rising throng of shouting voices. "I'll call Jack and get him to the office as soon as he can make it, but as you can appreciate, he's busy here and tonight is going to be something else. But he can at least get you up to speed. It's only right given that you're integral to the project."

Robert's ears pricked up at this, but he said nothing, not wanting to interfere with the dynamic of the project or interrupt Vicky's instructional flow.

"Meet me by the cashpoint in half an hour," said Vicky.

Robert nodded meekly and stood motionless, looking on as Vicky Hoyle's pert buttocks swung into the crowd and swiftly disappeared.

****

Vicky vanished into the crowd in the blink of an eye, leaving Robert and Fay being jostled by the ever-more fevered swarm. With the roads impassable and further reports emerging via social media of blockades of cars being formed across the entrances, there was no way of the police delivering riot squads by van. In light of the reception of the air ambulance, the clamouring throng had sent a statement to the world that they, as a collective – or at least a dominant number within that collective – did not want for there be any intervention, and they wanted neither help nor rescue. Despite this, news media coverage had trailed off and most earlier mentions were diminishing in umber. Robert began to speculate on whether or not some kind of media blackout was being effected. But it was clear that the people needed both help and rescue, and they also, more significantly, needed to be snapped out of the mania that was gripping them. It was as though they were in the clutches of some mass delusion, and Robert assumed that this was actually the case.

The question therefore came to centre around the precise nature of this mass delusion, in which people were loosing the shackles of societal norms to enter a freeform state of anomie. This was, Robert would later reflect at length, a true manifestation of Durkheim's depictions of a condition in which 'society provides little moral guidance to individuals' – a 'derangement', and 'an insatiable will'. The insatiable will of those who had descended upon Ebor Park simply seemed to be for material ownership, possession of possessions, and the possession of space. There was no suggestion of there being an end beyond this thirst for acquisition. And yes, he would also later reason, herd mentality gives rise to a normlessness that intimates an alternative set of norms. Just as anarchy can only exist fleetingly before a new order emerges, so an entire culture built around normlessness is predestined to undermine itself and eventually collapse. Anarchism will forever fail as a system by virtue of its absence of a system, and by the fact the very principle of anarchism is built around a rejection of society which is in itself a unifying alternative system, albeit one founded on antagonism. Put another way, Robert would summarise, in an anomic state, normlessness becomes the new norm.

As much as the baying horde was disunified and their objectives were entirely self-seeking, with their violent behaviour demonstrating an absolute disregard for anyone else, they were, perversely, unified in the fact they all displayed the same behaviours. What's more, in gravitating toward the shopping centre, they were revealing the same collectivism and conformity that lay at the heart of consumer culture in the first instance: everyone wants what everyone else wants or has, and no-one wants to be left behind. The ethos may be competitive, but it's collective, Robert would conclude in his draft report. This was no societal Brownian motion, but a reconfiguring of the mass mindset to a heightened level. Whatever Medico were engineering, it was seemingly designed to accentuate solipsistic and sociopathic tendencies, as well as disinhibit any predisposition to violence while at the same time promoting the desire for material acquisition.

Philanthropy was as dead as the medical crew, as those inside Asda continued to reinforce their barricades. Amid the commotion, Robert became suddenly aware of something new: cracks of what sounded like gunfire in the distance. He turned to see police on horseback, wearing visors and bullet-proof vests, firing into the more brutal knots of violence as they made their way into the retail park. He assumed these would be rubber bullets, but the first canister of tear gas to land in the middle of a particularly brutal brawl gave cause to reconsider given that such tactics were not licensed for British police. The scene unfurling more resembled a scene from CBS news: perhaps thirty or more people were engaged in combat, punching, kicking, biting, and fighting savagely, with no concern for their own preservation as hair was pulled and knees connected with noses, and trainer-tips with teeth, before the thick clouds of noxious smoke began pouring from the canister which landed in the midst of the bloody affray.

Retail Island

Robert grabbed Faye's arm and led her clumsily away through the baying crush in the vague direction of the cashpoint and the entrance to the tunnel. Along the way, he observed, albeit in a blur, a number of other faces he had seen around the Medico offices filming the scenes. He even clashed shoulders with a man who looked familiar, who was rushing in the opposite direction, toward the shot-firing, gas grenade-firing, mounted police, but was unable to identify him through the gas mask which covered his features bar his eyes.

****

It took Robert the best part of fifteen minutes to lead Fay to the cashpoint, which he noticed had in the last week seen the NatWest terminal replaced by a generic terminal illuminated in garish neon hues. Fay had been reluctant to accompany him, not being a part of the project and concerned over their connection being revealed to Jack Barham and his cohorts, but Robert had persuaded her with the argument that she was a Medico employee, and that her taking refuge in the office was about her safety rather than any personal proximity. For any employee to hide out while things escalated in the retail park would be justified.

En route, they passed a number of bloodied victims of the violent outbreaks which were becoming increasingly prevalent around the park. The bloodstains on the pavements, and the victims lying wounded, embedded themselves in Robert's mind as snapshots, images of reportage from a warzone or the wake of a riot scene. This didn't feel like real life, but instead resembled television, Internet. Robert was aware that as much as the gore turned his stomach, he felt little connection or compassion: the bodies lying strewn in the designated 'customer seating areas', in the doorways of less popular shops, and in random places around the flat expanse of the park, were simply characters in a movie. His detachment perturbed him, and Robert felt as if he was gradually slipping free of the shackles of humanity and transitioning toward an altogether different kind of existence, in which human emotion is but one more shade of the infinite spectrum of colour, rather than the dominant hue.

Robert felt Fay's fingers reach for his as they weaved their way through a succession of potential flashpoints. He took her hand, and gave a squeeze as their fingers interlaced. She shot him an anxious glance, her blue eyes darting as her gaze skipped to avoid the endless scenes of physical damage, of broken limbs and dented skulls, all inflicted in moments of mindlessness, and seemingly standing as evidence of the brutality of Medico's clinical explorations.

Vicky had eyed Fay with suspicion, and Robert noticed for the first time their physical similarity. Granted, they were a couple of inches different in height, but both were slender, well-proportioned, and with long, dark hair. If anything, Vicky resembled a polished, if slightly faded, CGI-tweaked fembot rendering of Fay, a Stepford Wife beside a real   (ex-)wife capable of unpredictable reactions and emotional depth. Robert remembered the iciness he felt from Vicky on their first encounter, the chill he had felt emanating from her clinical depthlessness.

Vicky lifted the manhole effortlessly – so effortlessly that Robert again began to question her biology – and waved first Fay, and then Robert, into the shaft. They had to hurry in order to avoid being observed, but night was falling, and a certain torpor was at last beginning to descend over the angry mob. But what concerned Robert was the fact that the mob was still there at all. It was nearing six pm, and instead of the crowds thinning as the shoppers made their way home for their evening meals and evenings spent watching pacifying reality TV, they continued to stream into the retail park, climbing over railings having walked from the cars they'd abandoned a mile or so up the road, despite the shops beginning to pull their shutters. Now, even more than ever, it was apparent that something was deeply wrong at Ebor Park.

Robert felt a sense of guilt swing around his belt-line as he took the first steps onto the metal ladder which descended below the retail park. He felt as if he were abandoning the stricken shoppers, clamouring like zombies toward the storefronts. They needed him... but what could he do? There was no question, in his heart of hearts, that someone needed to get to the root of this escalating insanity, and to put a stop to it.

But the first root he saw on walking through the almost deserted office belonged to John Cockram, and that root was surrounded by the saliva-coated lips of a trashy-looking blonde in her late twenties, with bobbed hair and burgundy lipstick, which was smeared around the base of his pulsating penis. In the empty office, he sat on a desk, trousers pulled around his ankles, while she gorged on his flesh. She was lean, perhaps a size eight to ten, her smart office trousers unzipped and slid down to reveal her buttocks, which Cockram was kneading with his fingertips, occasionally poking the tip of his middle finger into her puckered rectum. John didn't see Robert approaching as he had his eyes closed tight in a state of ecstasy, while the blonde being poked had her back to him, lashing his glistening tip and his saliva-soaked girth with her tongue. Robert wasn't sure how to react or where to walk, but decided to make as if nothing was happening and the office was still empty. The pair were so deeply immersed in their sex act that they seemed not to notice Robert as he drew near and slowly walked on past: her moss-green vest top and black bra were pulled down to reveal small, pointed breasts with elongated nipples – pale pink and a good three quarters of an inch in length – swaying as she serviced his stubby, circumcised penis.

Robert slipped by silently as John emitted a long sigh and spurted a hot stream of jissom over the woman's chest, which ran in thick, streaming rivulets over the mounds of her small breasts and channeled down through her cleavage. He averted his eyes as Cockram lapped the fluid off her long, spunk-dripping nipples and ran his tongue between her small breasts, all the while his hand working between her legs as she moaned crazily. As Robert made his way down the almost-deserted office in search of the designated meeting room – he and Vicky had exchanged numbers while at the cashpoint, and she had texted him the number of the meeting room she, Robert, and Jack were to meet at – he was aware of the blonde woman's moans growing in intensity and volume as she masturbated herself with an increasing tempo, finally bringing herself to climax as Cockram lapped at her juicing clitoris.

****

Retail Island

Robert felt as if they passed the scene in slow motion, and was aware that the voyeuristic arousal he experienced was inappropriate and misplaced. This awareness in turn introduced a new dimension to his simmering anxiety: the situation outside was increasingly tense and he was anxious that things could really flare up at any point – as if violence and the bringing down of an air ambulance didn't indicate things were already out of hand – but the sense that he was no longer fully in control of his own urges and impulses troubled him considerably.

Vicky had told Robert and Fay to wait in one of the office's 'breakout' areas – ostensibly a couple of high-backed sofas and a handful of brightly-coloured cube-shaped pouffes around an impractically low occasional table with a dazzling white laminate finish. Precisely what kind of mental wellbeing the company hoped to achieve with such misguided feng shui was unclear, and the pair sat restlessly and uncomfortably. Positioned side by side, they continually cast nervous sidelong glances at one another. Their body language reflected a mirror of growing anxiety. Robert noticed Fay's leg twitching nervously, and she constantly chewed the inside of her lip, while he gnawed at the skin around the base of the nails on his fingers and thumbs, stripping layers away until blood burst through the epidermis on his right thumb. Despite the fact the office was virtually deserted and the fact there was no-one within earshot, they spoke guardedly and in hushed tones.

"Why do I feel so churned up?" Fay asked in a whisper.

Robert shook his head, noticing that his knee was involuntarily jerking up and down rapidly too. He didn't speak, but simply raised an embarrassed eyebrow and gesticulated toward his twitching limb.

Instinctively, Fay extended a hand and rested it upon Robert's knee in an attempt to steady it, but to no avail. "What are we actually going to say?" she asked.

"I don't really know," Robert confessed. "I feel so lost and confused right now," he added, "This isn't like anything I've ever experienced before."

Just then, Vicky reappeared. "I've tracked Jack down and he's on his way," she said benignly but with a clipped, cooler undertone. "We should take this to somewhere more secluded, given the confidentiality of Project Mushroom."

Robert nodded and let her lead the way to one of the meeting rooms. "What's your precise involvement with the project?" he asked Vicky on the way.

"I'm essentially Jack's PA," she replied noncommittally.

"Essentially," Robert echoed, ponderously. "That's suitably vague, like everything else about the project. What level of disclosure does that grant you access to? Presumably everything that Jack's privy to?"

"Not everything," she replied cagily. She ushered the two of them into one of the medium-sized meeting rooms, and they seated themselves in the plush faux-leather chairs positioned around the oval smoked glass-topped table.

At that moment, Jack Barham breezed in, a broad, self-satisfied smile on his face, and, Robert detected, a certain glint in his eye which looked vaguely maniacal.

"Hello, hello," he gushed, rubbing his hands together. "And welcome to the next phase of Project Mushroom." It was abundantly clear that he was on the crest of a wave and pleased with the turn of events at the retail park.

Robert eyed him cautiously and noticed Vicky cast her eyes down with a supercilious look.

"Look," Robert said nervily, "perhaps we can cut the niceties and the bombast and talk about what the fuck is going on."

A flicker of surprise traced its way across Barham's physiognomy for a fleeting instant, but he immediately regained his composure and beamed amiably at his interlocutor. "Robert, Robert..." he said, emollient, placatory.

"Don't 'Robert' me," Ashton snapped, his temper fraying. "There are people seriously injured out there, there have been fatalities. You witnessed the scenes. I know because I saw you filming from the roof. And I've seen other Medico workers documenting the events. A helicopter's been brought down and its crew slaughtered, and seemingly all as part of some experiment. You think this is acceptable? What were you doing on the roof of the Primark unit when it was all kicking off?"

"My job," replied Jack evenly. "We all have a job to do."

"Yes, and members of firing squads and those charged with operating concentration camps had jobs to do, but this is the twenty-first century and you work for a pharmaceutical company. How can you possibly justify your job?"

"You may not believe it based on what you've witnessed, but these trials are for the greater good. You're not seeing the bigger picture, and right now I can't show you the bigger picture."

"I'm sorry, but does she have to be here?" Vicky interjected, indicating Fay with distain.

"Fay stays," Ashton snapped. "She's an employee and while she's not on the project, she's implicated by having borne witness to the scenes out there. People are behaving like animals, it's brutal and savage out there. Paint it how you like, but Medico has blood on its hands."

"Welcome to the world," nodded Barham with a bland smile. "If you can't see that the world is brutal and savage, then your days are numbered."

"But come on, this is not natural behaviour. And more to the point, you personally have blood on your hands. Are you comfortable living with that knowledge?"

"I think you'll find," Jack said dryly, and sidestepping Robert's last question, "that this is perfectly natural behaviour. The events at Ebor Park represent people returning to more primitive instincts. It's a case of dog eat dog. Only now, the competition isn't for food, but for consumables."

"This is fucked. People are actually dying," Robert persisted, his frustration mounting. "I think that's the bigger picture."

"You're mistaken." Barham said, evenly, even vaguely smugly, and Robert felt his hackles and his blood pressure rise. "A few lives are just collateral in any medical trial. Now, I agree, it has to be proportional. But this project is big enough to justify any collateral."

"No project is big enough," Robert retorted through grated teeth.

"No, really," replied Jack Barham almost expressionlessly. "This one is."

****

The first explosion shook the Medico office unexpectedly, and woke Robert from his slumber with a jolt. The second followed shortly after, and he saw Fay stirring in the flickering orange light that filtered through the gaps in the meeting room's Venetian blind. The pair had been advised to remain in the safe haven of the office rather than venture to their respective accommodation: transport toward town was practically non-existent on account of the jams, and the space between the office and the hotel had been deemed impassable by the authorities on account of volatile crowds having gathered along the route, and with a number of extremely violent incidents, even fatalities, having been reported on social media. Details were, however, sparse. While emergency services continued to be unable to reach the area – and Robert suspected they had decided to avoid making further efforts to venture to the area around Ebor Park for the safety of their crews – and he was now convinced there was a full media blackout around the developing situation, with the only updates trickling through social media rather than the mainstream networks. Posts – and even accounts – tended to mysteriously disappear, usually within minutes of being published. History was being not so much rewritten, but erased in real-time This was a cause for grave concern to Robert.

Jack's apparent dismissiveness of the escalating violence and the increasing potential for volatility had disturbed Robert, and he had been unconvinced by Barham's reassurances that the situation was in hand.

Retail Island

It was a fraction after one a.m. and instead of the crowds at the retail park dissipating, and heading home for their customary helpings of pre-prepared collation, they had remained and worked ever harder to hem themselves in during the hours since Robert and Fay had fled via the Medico tunnel. The reports filtering in, limited as they were, suggested that the traffic jam had achieved critical mass, extending some four miles or so in all directions on routes into the retail park. And yet, rather than abandon their journeys, the hundreds gravitating toward Ebor Park seemed to favour abandoning their vehicles, clambering in a zombie-like procession toward the retail mecca. The centre had seemingly acquired a magnetic quality, but Robert reflected that it perhaps resembled something of a honeytrap, luring the unsuspecting proletarians to a place of conflict, uncertainty, and potential destruction.

On hearing a loud crash and feeling tremors ripple through the room, Robert rushed to the window, while Fay lolled slowly from her slumber. He jerked the cord on the blinds to reveal a glowing vista, illuminated by orange hues. It wasn't easy to determine what had actually happened, but splitting the window ajar, he heard a tumult of shrieks, ranging from anger to anguish, confusion to pain. He continued to peer out into the night, struggling to make the detail against his reflection staring back at him.

"What is it?" Fay was finally lucid, having broken from her slumber.

"I'm not completely sure," Robert said, "but it looks like the shoppers have reinforced the blockades to the entrances to the park with busses, and set fire to them. I think the explosions were the petrol tanks of the two busses parked face to face across the entrance nearest us."

"Fuck," Fay gasped unguardedly.

"Fuck is right," Robert replied quietly. "If this is actually what's happened, then we're in a true siege situation."

"You should call Jack or Vicky," Fay said, stone-faced and scared-looking.

"It won't be news to them," Robert replied grimly. "This is precisely what they've engineered. That, or it's precisely what they need for their report, and they really are so disconnected on a human level that they don't care what happens. And I'm beginning to fear that this is the case. There's no limit on the collateral they're willing to expend."

Retail Island

Robert's first instinct was to run out of the office and see what damage had been done at the retail park: he was less concerned about the busses and the buildings than the bodies. He was alarmed by how ineffective the emergency services had been at reaching the location, but now, as he looked out of the window, he heard a heavy rumble build, and moments later saw the search beams of a military chinook scan the area. Soon, a second and a third Boeing CH-47 loomed into view through the darkness. The 30-metre, twin-engine, tandem-rotor, heavy-lift helicopters dominated the sky, the blades tearing at the dense atmosphere.

"Wait here," Robert told Fay, swallowing his anxiety as a surge of adrenaline took hold of his system. He tugged at his shirt, embarrassed fleetingly by his dishevelment, before realising she was stroking at her hair and moving hands over her own garments, as if appearances mattered under the circumstances.

"Please don't leave me on my own" she said, timorously.

Fleetingly, he held her gaze, fixing her sharp blue eyes on his, taking in her pale face and straight, dark hair. He felt her panic reach to his lower abdomen, and understood her fear.

"You're safer here," he countered. "I think this could be the beginning of the end game, and I need to find Jack."

Robert felt acid bile rise in his gullet. He felt nowhere near as brave as he was presenting, but this was by no means only for Fay's benefit as a cliché display of masculine strength: he had to reclaim a pocket of his old self and former capacity for himself and his sanity.

"Fuck's sake," Fay shot at him, suddenly irritated and frustrated by the accentuation of her limitations. "I'm not that feeble, you know."

Robert took a long, deep breath. "I'm not saying that. I'm just saying I need you to be safe. We don't know what some of these people are capable of, and we don't need both of us to be running around separately. We could easily each sabotage the other quite by accident."

Hunter acquiesced with a disconsolate sigh, her head falling forwards and her hair hanging, defeated as she exhaled. She didn't speak but merely shrugged her slender shoulders.

"Besides," Ashton added before he left, "I need your eyes. Keep an eye on the scene here and keep me posted."

They watched for another minute as the first of the 24,578lb helicopters lowered itself and hovered only a short way above the jostling mob, and soldiers began to leap like lemmings from the vehicle onto the smooth tarmac below. As they watched, a flare flew through the sky and into the side of the transporter. With a retina-searing flash of orange and white, the Chinook burst into flames and crumpled to the ground in very much the same way as the medical rescue vehicle before it.

Robert and Fay stood at the window, jaws dropping in unison. A vast orange plume erupted like a volcano from the immense grey hulk as the bodies of soldiers flew from the open side.

"What was that?" gasped Fay.

"Looked very like a ground to air missile to me, and it was fired from this building."

****

Nosnibor

Retail Island

The meeting room suddenly felt extremely claustrophobic as the realisation hit that just a few partition walls stood between them and a cold-blooded killer armed with heavy military-grade artillery.

Outside, the other two helicopters had remained on the far side of the retail complex, beyond the range of what Robert assumed was a portable shoulder-launching MANPADS rather than anything larger. They hovered above the cars, packed solid in the Asda car park, and Robert could just make out, illuminated by floodlights and the helicopters' search beams, the soldiers descending into the crowd like ants swarming down into an open jam pot.

It seemed as if there were two very different end-games playing out simultaneously, and Robert was torn between which of the two he should engage with. He was no longer certain of his precise position on the project on behalf of Medico: Project Mushroom seemed increasingly like the most dangerous clusterfuck he had ever been party to, and the whole thing felt completely surreal. At the same time, despite being employed by Medico to work on Project Mushroom, and contracted to report on its outcomes, he also felt a societal and civic responsibility to blow the whistle on Medico and its dangerous practices. This would be in direct contravention of his NDA. Robert was torn, and the uprising of anxiety broke a heavy perspiration on his brow, torso and back. The awareness of his increasing fragility set a marker which perpetuated a typical cycle, and he began to anxietise about his anxiety. He gripped Fay by the wrist, his hand slick and clammy, and then began to anxietise that this was possibly unusual and potentially inappropriate.

She looked at him, her eyes wide but understanding, and he realised the establishment of their non-verbal connection ran deep.

They locked in a stare for a fleeting moment, and in the silence of the glass-walled room he could hear her accelerated breathing.

"We need to find who fired the missile," Robert said, evenly, even as his heart was palpating.

****

Robert made his way out of the meeting room, leaving Fay with instructions to stay put, keep an eye on happenings outside, and to try to make contact with Vicky and anyone else who may be able to help locate Jack and to bring things back under control. While the military presence on the ground would likely help bring things down to a calmer level around Asda and the far side of Ebor Park, the hulk of the burning helicopter near Primark had only increased the rioting frenzy, and figures could plainly be seen in silhouette against the dazzling luminescence of the inferno, lashing out in every direction. A thick tower of acrid black smoke had risen into the night sky, adding layers of darkness upon darkness. The scene resembled some kind of retail apocalypse.

In the event, it was Robert who found Jack. Making his way down the corridor in the direction he believed the missile had originated, judging by the arc of its trajectory toward the helicopter, he peered through the door of each room along the way – a series of conference rooms and demonstration spaces, as well as a couple of relaxation hubs and storage cupboards. The seventh room along was a spacious meeting room decked out with an immense screen for videoconferencing. The main lights were off, meaning only vague silhouetted shapes were discernible in the low-level night lighting. Robert stuck his head around the door and surveyed the scene, and took a moment to identify a figure standing in the far corner, his back pressed against the wall. The flicker of the flames partially illuminated one side of Jack Barham's face as he looked, side-on, out of the window which occupied the entire wall from floor to ceiling.

Robert caught his breath: he wasn't sure what to say, or even whether he should speak. Jack, however, had seen the light from the corridor illuminate the room's entrance

"Robert?" he called out in a cracked whisper.

"Jack?" Robert returned superfluously, mirroring Barham's hushed tone.

"Come in. Leave the lights off. It's important no-one sees us."

Tentatively, Robert approached. "Jack... the helicopter..."

"I know."

"The missile..." Robert was floundering. He took a deep intake of breath and blew out sharply in an attempt to focus himself and regain his composure. His mouth felt dry, already certain of the answer to the question he couldn't bring himself to ask even as he noticed the hand-held rocket launcher propped against the wall.

"I had to, Robert," Jack said evenly, pre-empting it.

"I can't see that," Robert replied. "Things were already out of hand before. People are getting killed out there. And now you've actually taken down a military aircraft, killing possibly dozens in the process... for what? This is beyond madness, and it has to stop."

"That's where you're wrong," Barham said, his voice growing more confident and airy. "This is nowhere near the end."

"Christ, what the fuck is wrong with you?" Robert demanded, his fury and desperation suddenly taking hold. He grabbed Barham by the collar and rammed him, hard, against the wall. He had no idea what he was aiming to achieve, only that he had to find a way to get through to the man.

He felt a white-hot explosion of pain burst in his jaw as Jack's fist made contact, throwing him reeling backwards and stumbling over some chairs before his trajectory was halted by the table which centred the room. "And what the fuck is wrong with *you*?" Barham barked, hoarse-throated with rage.

Robert steadied himself and considered his next move. "Listen," he said, trying to contain the tremble in his voice. "We need to talk. If you won't stop this insanity, I have no choice but to do it myself, for the sake of people's lives."

"You don't understand," replied Jack. "What we're doing is for the sake of even more lives, ultimately."

"Maybe you'd better make me understand," said Ashton. "Or otherwise stop me. I have contacts."

"No need to make threats," Barham said, unctuously. "Even if I'm not convinced you could necessarily fulfil them, I know better than to underestimate the power of determination. So, where should I begin? While, as I've said, and as is a condition of your contract, information concerning Project Mushroom is only disclosed on a need-to-know basis. But it's starting to look like you need to know before you derail things. I'm prepared to invite you to tomorrow's project meeting."

"Invitation accepted, although I also have some questions beforehand."

"Fire away."

"Well, you already did that," Robert said sarcastically. "But ok. First. The tunnel. How come?"

"Ah," said Jack with the vaguest hint of a conspiratorial smile. "Ebor Park has a number of interesting features, of which the tunnel is only one. These include special access to rooftop surveillance points..."

"Like the one I saw you at on top of the Primark unit?" Robert interjected.

"Like the one you saw me at on top of the Primark unit," Jack affirmed, "along with CCTV installed in what may be considered unconventional locations throughout the park, including all of the retail units. And all of the retail units have customised air-conditioning filters, which are also inbuilt at strategic zones around the car park and so on."

"But why? How come?" Ashton challenged.

Jack sighed and began speaking as though to a child who was struggling with the concept of the universe. "Because we needed a place to conduct these experiments. Project Mushroom is immense in its scope, and is just over four years into a twelve-year plan. As the name suggests, it spreads, rhizome-like, under the ground."

"Nice concept," Robert conceded. "But are you really saying...?"

"What I'm saying is that Medico funded the construction of Ebor Park. It's essentially custom-built as a test centre. It's a living laboratory. And in glorious synergy, because we own it, the rent the retailers pay on the units comes directly back to fund the project." Barham was fully beaming now.

"If this is true, it's the most dangerous and insidious thing I've ever encountered," said Ashton, horrified. "It's often said that the pharmaceutical firms like to play God, but..."

"Yes," Jack nodded smugly, "and we're actually living the dream."

****

Retail Island

The meeting was scheduled for 9am sharp. Jack Barham had been reluctant to grant Fay an invitation, but finally bowed to Robert's pressure. On arrival at 08:48, accompanied by Fay Hunter, Robert Ashton surveyed the delegates already present and found most of the faces were already familiar to him. Fiona Dexter and Samantha Bertram sat side by side in thin, colourful, summery-patterned dresses, backs straight and shooting sidelong glances at one another as if they were competing to see which could show off their bust to the greatest effect. Phil Thomson and Janice Smythe were deep in animated conversation and failed to acknowledge Robert and Fay's arrival.

The young guy with a quiff whom Robert had seen at a previous meeting sat in a slim-fitting shirt and shiny, skinny-fit grey suit that wasn't well-suited to his burgeoning pot-belly – Robert could see that his name was Alex Greenbaum – was seated beside a young brunette in her early twenties. The ID card which swung from her Medico-branded lanyard revealed her name to be Corrine Davies. She wore a strappy black vest top, and Robert observed a certain similarity to both Fay and Vicky Hoyle, although she was smaller-chested, and had a slight olive hue to her skin, which may or not have been artificial.

Retail Island

Also present was a plump, middle-aged woman with straw-blonde hair who chuckled a lot and talked unnecessarily about shoes and diets, seemingly in an attempt to detract from the fact she had nothing of substance to contribute to the project; a fat bloke in his forties; another fat bloke in his fifties, balding and bored-looking; and a thick-set guy whose shirt was too tight, who rambled inanely and in autistic detail about nothing of consequence. A shrewish-looking woman of indeterminate age, who was wearing a misshapen floral charity-shop dress, completed the lineup.

Ashton and Hunter assumed seats at a far corner of the vast glass-topped table as discreetly as possible. Robert sensed an increasingly familiar tension in the room's atmosphere and was determined to keep Fay as close as possible, for both their sakes. He sensed that they served to shield one another from whatever strangeness was in the air.

John Cockram slipped into the room, accompanied by the trashy-looking blonde in her late twenties, whom they had witnessed him engaged in a sex act with on their arrival at the office via the tunnel. Robert noticed that her bleached blonde bob looked disheveled and her cheeks flushed, while Cockram looked sweaty and flustered.

At precisely 08:58, Jack Barham breezed in, shadowed by Vicky Hoyle, and proceeded to assume his premier position at the head of the table with Hoyle. Vicky looked more porcelain and robotic than ever, as she sat to his immediate right with her back as straight as a rod. The babble of chatter which had previously filled the expansive space fell silent the second Barham raised his hands. He surveyed the delegates, one by one, in a nonchalant and commanding fashion.

"It's been an eventful twenty-four hours," he announced, somewhat redundantly. "I'd like to welcome two new additions to the inner sanctum of Project Mushroom: Robert Ashton and Fay Hunter." He extended a besuited sleeve in the guests' direction and the other delegates turned and nodded acknowledgement. Robert and Fay nodded back around the table, making their best efforts not to look uncomfortable.

Barham gave a brief but bombastic preamble by way of a fudged explanation of their presence on account of their supposed contribution to the latest phase of the project, before giving a recap of the week's events which likely went over the heads of many of those present. The presentation was complete with graphs, charts and near-infinite statistics and figures. He asked if there were any questions: there were few, and they were all extremely technical in nature, and couched in obscure phraseology: Barham's responses were equally impenetrable, laden with jargonistic industry terminologies and off-kilter theoretical references to the psychology of consumerism.

"But of course, perhaps this all has more impact and meaning if we actually review the real results," Jack said, rounding off his lengthy introduction and the somewhat fatuous-seeming Q&A session which had followed. He flicked another button and the screen changed. "Please, step forward. This is exactly what we've achieved these last few days. I'd like to thank you all for your contributions."

On the screen, which stood the full height and width of one of the room's shorter sides – some ten feet high and still fully thirty feet wide – footage of the escalating violence hove into view. Robert immediately recognised the clips as having been shot by the various Medico employees he had observed stationed around the retail park, as some of the shots he had witnessed first-hand, while seeing the likes of Vicky Hoyle, Tom Grindstaff, and Steve Thompson looking on, impassively, smart phones in hand capturing events as they unfolded. There was also footage obtained from the myriad CCTV cameras located inside the stores. The quality of the footage was outstanding, and Jack made mention of the fact that the camera system was the most hi-check kit going, and that they monitored activity in stores remotely from 'the bunker', an underground office in the basement of the Medico office, with no fewer than 100 screens which received real-time streams from surveillance around the park.

At first, only a handful of the delegates had risen from their seats, but slowly, the rest got up and inched nearer to the screen, huddling closer as if to fill their entire vision with the scenes of flying fists and shoes, clothes and hair being pulled, bricks and other missiles being hurled and fires being lit. Robert sensed Fay beginning to stir. He caught her arm and shot a cautionary look directly into her blue eyes. She slowly closed her long-lashed lids and returned her spine to the back of the leather-bound chair. They looked on as the other delegates pressed closer to one another: Robert noticed that Alex Greenbaum had snaked an arm around Corrine Davies' waist; this gradually made its way down until his hand was first resting on, then gently caressing, and eventually beginning to kneed at her left buttock. Through the gathering, Robert could also see that Phil Thompson was rubbing the nape of Janice Smythe's neck; she squirmed with a shiver of pleasure. The atmosphere had changed. Something was beginning to happen.

Samantha Bertram inched a hand up inside Fiona Dexter's hemline and began to massage her inner thigh, slowly working her way upwards. Robert felt his breathing quicken and he shot Fay another look, and witnessed a look of surprise slowly fixing onto her pretty, pale face. She arched an eyebrow and gave an expression of deep discomfort. Bertram and Dexter inched back through the cluster of screen-watchers, until they reached the glass-topped table. Samantha slid herself up onto it, and pulled her dress down to reveal her ample mammaries with their enormous nipples, and she kneeded them ecstatically as Fiona pulled her knickers down and worked feverishly at her juicing clitoris.

Corrine Davies wasn't wearing any knickers. Alex Greenbaum had lifted her khaki denim miniskirt to reveal her smooth buttocks and was working a finger in and out of her anus as she squirmed with rapturous delight. And so the scene unfolded: Tom Grindstaff unbuckled his belt and unzipped his fly to expose his pulsating member. He climbed onto the table on top of Fiona Dexter, rubbing his glans the length of her spine and smearing a silvery trail through her hair, before arriving at Sam Bertram; she eagerly took his glistening tip between her lips before gorging herself greedily on the fullness of his six-inch length.

Swapping, Sam took Alex's balls fully in her mouth and simultaneously worked Jack Barham's meat with her hand, while Jack suckled on Vicky Hoyle's shiny, pale pink, saliva-coated nipples. Janice Smythe and the trashy blonde were taking turns on Phil Thompson's throbbing phallus, a string of ejaculate trailing between their glazed, ruddied faces.

It was an ever-shifting mass of moaning flesh, as partners swapped over and over: the mousy thrift-shop nerd had her floral dress pulled down to reveal sagging dugs with elongated brown nipples, the areolae stretched large over tits tracked with silvery stretch-marks as she sat on the lap of the fat bloke in his forties with her skirt hitched to her hips. Fiona approached her and grasped her by the lank brown hair, plunging her horsey visage into her heaving, perspiring cleavage. The mousey woman bucked and began to savagely lap and chew at the angry nipples that had been thrust into her face, before the thick-set guy whose tight shirt was now undone and his trousers nowhere to be seen, slipped his uncircumcised member between her buttocks and began to pound her dripping vagina.

The scenes of violence, bloodshed and brutality continued to play out on the screen before them, the close-up shots of heavy blows and blossoming contusions, open wounds and cries of agony as flames seared flesh providing the optimally juxtaposed backdrop to the frenzy of the flesh being enacted with wild abandon in the meeting room. The dual scenes resembled some perverse and oddly-choreographed ballets. As he guided Fay silently out of the room in search of safe haven, Robert reflected that in some way, the scenes inside the meeting room bore a strange similarity to those equally savage and primal acts portrayed on screen, and which continued to play in real-time outside in the retail park.

****

Part 3: Departures

Robert figured that accessing any files pertaining to Project Mushroom that he possibly could would be the next most instructional course of action, although, he reflected as he sat beside Fay at her desk, this morning's scenes had been highly informative in themselves. Fay's access to files was restricted, but she was able to access staff contacts which were unavailable to Robert. Robert, in turn, was able to use the laptop he had been loaned for the duration of his contract to facilitate access to a select range of project-related files and dossiers. Between them, they were still able to build a tree of the origins of the various staff involved in Project Mushroom, including the faces Robert had been unable to name.

The fat bloke in his fifties, balding and bored-looking, whom Robert had spotted a couple of times was Leonard Harpington, a chemical engineer, while the shrewish-looking woman of indeterminate age who favoured charity-shop clothes, who had proven herself to be a truly vociferous lover despite her demur and overtly nerdy appearance and varicose veins, was a prominent physicist who also specialised in the physics of psychology. Her name was Elspeth

Boonbrook, and she had previously worked, according to her staff resumé, for the US government in a capacity which was not disclosed and, they assumed, was non-disclosable. It soon became clear that collectively, the operatives on Project Mushroom had the potential to be dangerous on a pan-continental scale, and that Jack Bahram's claim that it could spread to become something truly vast while remaining largely underground was not the hot air Robert had first thought, and would have liked to have believed.

Ashton's access was limited to the pockets of the project he needed to know about, which it had been evident from the outset. It was comparatively little in the scheme of things.

"I can't help but feel a sense of futility here," he said, realising just how badly his hands were trembling. His breaths were short, and it dawned on him that he was displaying the physical symptoms of a mild panic attack.

"Me too," Fay said, the despondency in her voice laced with a heavy hint of anxiety. "What we need to do is gain access to Jack's account..."

"I hadn't thought of that," snapped Robert sarcastically.

"No need to be like that," Fay sniped. "I may *actually* have a way."

Robert raised his eyebrows, a mix of surprise and disbelief. And, assuming Fay was able to deliver, a prefatory pang of guilt for underestimating her also prodded at Robert's troubled psyche. "Why didn't you say so sooner?"

"I've only just got there. I've been digging. Managed to swipe this off Vicky in the tunnel," Fay said with a wickedly triumphant grin as she lofted a secondary pass-card bearing Jack Barham's credentials and a USB memory stick.

"What? How?"

Fay blushed a little and shook her head, looking embarrassed. "Let's just see what we can get now, ok?"

Robert nodded silently as he accepted the proffered ID card. Marked 'secondary user', it contained a reduced-sized mug-shot of Jack Barham, and granted Vicky, as his assistant, access to his files. On the card's reverse were various serial numbers and passcodes, and Robert was able, after a number of attempts, to gain access to the labyrinthine data folders for Project Mushroom on Medico's servers. While he trawled blindly, Fay browsed the contents of the memory stick, and as she did so, copied its contents to a stick of her own. "I think I've got a few bits," she whispered.

"Good. Me too. We need to get as much as we can, and as quickly as we can, and get out of here before they find us." Robert busied himself copying as much as he could to a memory stick he carried in his jacket pocket. His hands and brow were hot and sweaty and perspiration began to run from his armpits down inside his shirt. He began to feel dizzy, and flickering images of gaping flesh wounds and thudding fists shot in hyper-zoomed close-up, alternating with images of the teeming fuckfest they had born witness to, replayed in his mind while the text of documents classified as secret swam before his eyes.

On hearing the first voices emerge from the meeting room, Ashton slammed his laptop shutand gestured to Fay to grab the memory stick.

"I'm not done," she rasped in irritation.

"We'll have to use what we've got," Robert whispered hoarsely. "They're coming."

Right on cue, Leonard Harpington rounded the corner of the corridor onto the main floor of the open-plan office.

Nosnibor

"Where are we going?" Hunter hissed.

"Stay down and follow me."

****

Retail Island

Back at Robert's hotel room, they cracked open a bottle of wine to unwind and began to trawl through the documents they had pillaged. While neither would admit it to themselves or the other, there felt something vaguely naughty, not just about the datatheft, but the simple act of sitting side by side on a small settee in a hotel room. It had been quite a battle to the hotel. Ordinarily they may have taken a taxi, but the road was completely jammed. By now, around half of the cars stood empty, abandoned. The people who remained with their vehicles were tense, angry, and hungry, and in an ugly, aggressive mood. Consequently, although the roadside journey had taken a mere twenty-three minutes, it had been treacherous, and the walk had been interrupted by a succession of people, mainly burly, beer-gutted men in T-shirts, demanding to know where they were going, and why. Their suspicion was hard to take, and Robert made a mental note of escalating paranoia as a prevailing symptom of those present in both Medico and Ebor Park.

In Robert's room, they waded through endless files, scanning reams of documents and data relating to various pheromones being filtered into the office through the air-conditioning. There were endless transcripts of conversations held at one-to-one meetings between managers and their staff about heightened sexual arousal around colleagues, and verbatim accounts of unexpected and inappropriate interactions with fellow members of staff. The number of initiators and recipients was approximately equal, and reading through the accounts, even encounters which began as non-consensual rapidly became consensual, and as such, no reports of any improper conduct, let alone sexual harassment or rape, had been made. And yet they had witnessed, with their own eyes, acts of depravity to rival de Sade. The cocktail of chemicals pumped into the building clearly contained more than pheromones, but what precisely was in the air which put such complete blocks on normalised behaviours wasn't immediately apparent from the documents they had in their possession. Focusing on the matter at hand, and the vast mass of data they held, illicitly, neither contemplated the question of their own apparent immunity from this particular extreme and deviant experiment which it appeared was directed toward all employees of the Medico office at Ebor Park.

The room was riven with potentialities on which neither would act, but of which they were both overwhelmingly aware. Arms, shoulders, hips, thighs and ankles pressed together, they hunched over Robert's compact laptop, jaws by turn clenched and agape as they surveyed the information they had netted. They opened a second bottle of wine.

"We could actually go to prison for this," Fay said, chewing her lip nervously.

Robert nodded gravely, discomfort embracing his body. "We could get fucking David Kelly'd for this," he said darkly.

Fay's eyes widened for a moment. "Don't say that," she muttered, taking a deep hit on the glass of wine in her hand.

"Look, this is bigger than we'd realised," Robert said, trying to mask the desperation in his voice. "Let's look at the facts. Ebor Park is funded by Medico. It got planning permission with all of its weird additions and details. Riots kick off and help is slow to arrive. In fact, it's barely even a gesture of help. The military turn up and a helicopter gets blown out of the sky. It's obvious where the missile was fired from, but do you see the military storming the Medico office? Have they sent in the drones to take out the shooter? Have they bombed the fuck out of the place? No. Why not?"

Fay cast her eyes downwards and nursed her glass in both hands. "Fucking hell," she muttered. "Is there anyone or any agency not complicit in this?" she muttered.

"Probably not," Robert conceded. "I don't think we can actually win this. When I mentioned MK Ultra, I had no idea..."

"We can't win, can we?" Fay asked, looking disconsolate. "With so many 'experts', the military, *and* the government on-side, whatever we do, we'll be dismissed as conspiracy theorist nutters." She picked up the wine and poured them each another large glass.

Robert sighed. His chest and limbs felt heavy as he cast his increasingly bleary eyes over a document which confirmed the government's backing of Medico and Project Mushroom. "Pretty much," he said a tightness binding his throat. "We've got it right here. Even any military losses are deemed justifiable collateral given the scope of the project. Put simply, Medico put enough into the coffers to justify any cost. They pay tariffs to the government which buy their backing; they pay taxes, albeit with massive breaks for mass distribution of their mass inoculations, and they receive two-way kickbacks with their drugs being on prescription lists. Medico scratches the government's back scratches Medico's back scratches the government's back..."

"Fuck's sake." Suddenly, Fay looked tired. Her face turned pale, her eyebrows wilted and her body sagged into Robert's. She sank the last of her wine and settled close into him on the sofa.

He placed his arm around her shoulder and drew her close. Robert felt cold and tired and needed her there beside him. Fay began to nod off, and so did Robert, before he was suddenly jolted by the trill and buzz of his mobile. It was Jack Barham.

Robert shook the wine haze from his head and picked up the phone, suddenly sober. He took the call.

"Jack? It's nearly midnight."

"Yes, sorry," Jack blustered on the other end of the line, his deep but jarring breaths suggesting he was engaged in sexual activity. "Something I need to show you." He halted and stuttered a second, breathing erratically. "My office at nine tomorrow morning... ok?"

"I suppose so," replied Robert, and immediately the line went dead.

Fay had roused from her sleep by the time Robert ended the brief call. The wine exhausted, Robert lifted a bottle of vodka from his suitcase and raised it in an offering gesture. Fay nodded and he poured them each a generous measure into the wine glasses they had been using. They raised a silent toast with the pink-hued spirit and sank the shots in one.

****

"What is it, Jack? You actually sounded quite flustered last night," Robert began on entering Jack's office. He had decided that playing the cautious, concerned, yet forward card was probably the better option over either a confrontational or timid approach, but the fact was Ashton had no idea as to how best approach Barham after witnessing his behaviour over the last fortnight or so. Jack Barham was as much an enigma as the project he was fronting.

Barham looked a shade edgy, and above all, weary. "Thanks for coming, Robert." Despite it all, he maintained his breezy, professional demeanour, and Robert couldn't help but notice how crisply pressed his shirt and suit looked, especially in comparison to the crumpled kit he was sporting: his jacket and trousers were a week in and had spent the nights – when not being worn overnight in meeting rooms – in a heap in the corner on the floor of various rooms. "I think you've already deduced we're reaching a certain turning point in the project, and I'd like to begin by thanking you for your contribution."

"I really don't feel as if I've done all that much," Robert said, blandly. "And that sounds very much like you're about to show me the door."

Jack exhaled long and slow through his nostrils, and Robert watched his barrelled chest deflate gradually. "Not at all," Barham assured him. "You underrate your input," he added, his eyes closed and his head nodding slowly.

Robert couldn't help but think what a pretentious prick Barham was in this moment, the epitome of corporate slime. "Let's cut the shit, Jack," he said, suddenly frustrated. "What's the deal?"

Jack was genuinely taken aback by Robert's forthright challenge, and momentarily bletched. He swerved and diverted, buying himself time: "You and

Fay Hunter seem to be getting along well," he remarked archly.

"Irrelevant," snapped Robert defensively. "But..." he hesitated, "since you raise the issue, at least indirectly. She and I seem to be the only ones not in permanent heat in this office." He paused and let the silence hang for a few pregnant moments. "The irony isn't lost," he added dryly.

Barham twitched: it seemed the irony wasn't found. "I think I should probably show you something," he said. "Let's go."

****

Having returned to the retail park via the tunnel and taken a secret back-route around the units in order to ultimately gain access to the rooftop surveillance platform above Primark, Robert looked on aghast and Jack beamed expansively as the pair surveyed the scene below. Robert felt a sickness in the pit of his stomach at the sight of mass brawling and unconscious bodies bleeding on the ground. The pother had been frothing for a full fortnight now, and despite making the national news on many evenings in the first week, the scenes at Ebor Park had swiftly dropped off the radar when there had been a machine-gun killing spree at Meadowhall. Just as Derek Bird's Cumbrian massacre had rapidly been usurped by Raol Moat in the rolling news feeds, so it was possible that an inexplicable state-sponsored riot situation with fatalities well into double figures could be swiftly eclipsed by something with lower impact but a more linear narrative that made for juicier reportage.

To return to the comparison: Bird killed twelve and injured eleven in a day-long killing spree. But in killing himself he killed the story. Moat, on the other hand, on the run and with a twist added by addled alcoholic football veteran Paul Gascoigne offering support, gave rolling news an unfolding narrative flow over the longer stretch. And so it was that the UK's biggest mass-killing, ranking alongside the 1987 Hungerford massacre, the 1989 Monkseaton shootings, and the 1996 Dunblane school massacre, was forgotten due to a half-wit who claimed only three lives but made for more engaging television.

The entrance to the retail park, to the right of the vast end unit as they looked down, was still blockaded by a pair of busses jammed end to end, parked sideways across the slip-road. Both had burned out to blackened shells, and the flames had died down to a low glow from within. Even so, a pall of acrid black smoke continued to rise from the empty rectangles where windows once hung, and the charred hulks, pushed to dangerous angles, still black and menacing despite having been slain, providing a stark message that no-one was welcome to enter the ark, and similarly, departure was not permitted either.

A scattering of army troops was visible among the seething masses but they didn't seem to be making any concerted attempt to do anything other than perpetuate age-old cliché steretypes of offering a menacing presence as they stood, arms on display and jaws clenched.

"What are you actually showing me, beyond a riot that's been raging for a fortnight?" Robert asked, fully aware.

Barham looked around. "I'm showing you this," he said, his arms extending around the entire scene.

Ashton looked down, and immediately wished he hadn't. He felt dizzy. Moreover, thirty feet below, the ruckus continued unabated, with fists and feet flying every which way, and blood staining the ground.

"What do you notice?" asked Jack with disconcerting glee.

"I notice that you seem to be really enjoying this," shot back Robert dryly.

"Of course I am," Jack beamed breezily. "But..." he added after a pause, "anything else?"

"What am I looking for? The whole situation is perverse," Robert snapped. This was not the line of project work he was accustomed to, and he felt deeply uncomfortable.

"These people aren't raiding or looting," Barham said with pride.

"The ones at Asda would be if the doors hadn't been barricaded. We have no idea what's going on inside. And besides, so... so what? They're still rioting, they're still damaging property and one another. There have been deaths. Look, there are bodies bleeding on the ground."

As they watched, troops who had arrived in the two helicopters that had now managed to land on the wasteland on the other side of the link road were making their way through the seething mass of battered brawlers and dragging the broken corpses out of the way, lugging them through the rammed car park towards Clinton's Cards. The space in front of this unit, at the farthest corner of the park from both Primark and Asda, was clear of people, meaning that the bodies could be laid out on the wide walkway.

"Yes, and that's on one hand regrettable, but on the other, a mark of Mushroom's success."

"So you've created a chemical which can trigger a riot situation. Well done. But what does it prove?"

"Not a chemical. A frequency. The frequency is actually being emitted by the Primark unit. It has a directional transmission, and a specific targeted reach of approximately one hundred and twenty feet. You'll note that the riot zone is almost a perfect rectangle, the width of the Primark unit and extending back by around, oh, a hundred and twenty feet. Look, the point is, we can manipulate, absolutely, the behaviours of large numbers of individuals at once, to create a collective behavioural change. These people aren't remotely interested in material goods – I mean, they are here for them, but the frequency hasn't interfered with their moral compass. They won't steal or loot. They will kill one another to get into the store and to get their hands on the goods, but they'll pay for them on principle."

Robert felt his breath catch in his chest. He felt a sudden rising impulse to act, and it struck him with a stark clinicality just how easy it would be to launch Jack Barham off the surveillance platform and down to the paved ground below, leaving him to the mercy of the violent mob – assuming he survived the fall. Instead, he asked, "Is that it?" Not waiting for a response he continued as questions began to stream into his mind. "But why are they out here on *en masse* anyway?"

Jack looked at him with a mixture of surprise and perplexity. "Shopping, of course," he said, an incredulous and patronising edge to his tone. "A new discount clothing store... they came here of their own accord. This is the reality of post-millennial consumer culture. But now... I want to show you something else."

****

Retail Island

"It's all about frequencies," Jack said as he led Robert through a series of tunnels and passages. "We've combined the research that gave us medical ultrasound with the work done by the US military to develop ultrasonic weapons with a view to modifying and controlling behaviour in large groups. We know that studies have found that exposure to high intensity ultrasound at frequencies from 700 kHz to 3.6 MHz can cause lung and intestinal damage in mice. Heart rate patterns following vibroacoustic stimulation has resulted in serious negative consequences such as atrial flutter and bradycardia. We know that the extra-aural bioeffects of certain frequencies on various internal organs and the central nervous system include auditory shifts, vibrotactile sensitivity change, muscle contraction, cardiovascular function change, central nervous system effects, vestibular effects, and chest wall/lung tissue effects. Research has found that low frequency sonar exposure could result in significant cavitations, hypothermia, and tissue shearing."

"This goes a long way beyond the 'brown' note," Robert remarked dryly. "But yes, I am aware of this. It was also reported that 'sonic attacks' may have taken place in Cuba in 2016 and 2017, leading to health problems, including hearing loss in US and Canadian government employees at the US and Canadian embassies in Havana. But these were dismissed as an example of mass psychogenic illness on account of the facts concerning about the alleged attacks seemingly violating the laws of physics."

"Physics has moved on apace," Jack said, a twinkle in his eye. "And of course the voracity of those reports was called into question and the explanations dismissed as conspiracy. Can you imagine if word actually got out?"

Robert winced inwardly at his relentless bravado, but accepted the suggestion that Project Mushroom was pushing science in directions which seemed beyond possibility.

"Those sonic attacks happened, and they were real, and the effects were real. I *did* tell you that Project Mushroom was global, didn't I?"

Jack led Robert to another rooftop surveillance post, this time above Asda. The scene below was again brutal. This had evolved differently, with looting and brazen shoplifting in abundance. A number of those who had barricaded themselves in had been broken out as the sheer number desperate to make their way into the store gradually overwhelmed them, barraging the glass doors at first with bricks and pieces of paving slab and curb stone, followed later by primitive incendiary devices and even various attempts at ram-raiding the store, with some success.

"And what do you notice here?" asked Jack, his chest puffing with pride.

Again, Robert envisioned himself dragging the dangerous, messianic figure over the precipice and casting him to the ground below. Ashton shook his head, incapable of speech. Jack's arrogant grin fuelled Robert's now white-hot rage.

"More blood. More fighting. What am I looking for?" Robert was growing exasperated.

"The people who barricaded themselves in are being besieged by people who want in. Some have got in and are leaving with expensive goods and large quantities of food."

"Right..."

"Different frequency. Different effects," said Jack, smugly.

"Can you really take the credit for that? Isn't there a predisposition in a consumer society to take what you can't afford when the opportunity presents itself?" Robert challenged.

"Yes, but we blocked the frequencies from Primark to prevent cross-contamination. And while the looting and thieving is actually normal human behaviour, the fighting is less so. And that's what we've engineered. As much as we're a pharmaceutical company, you might say that Medico is a biological engineering company."

"*You* might say that," Ashton retorted as they surveyed the scene. "But the whole thing is deranged."

"To paraphrase Deleuze and Guattari, derangement is the only sane response to an insane society. With Project Mushroom, Medico are looking to channel and harness that derangement to bring about a new social order."

Robert shrugged in defeat as the military men who had infiltrated the space continued in their failure to bring the situation under control. Gripped once more by an overwhelming urge, he turned to Jack and gripped him by the lapels. He relished the look of terror as it flooded over the corporate megalomaniac's self-satisfied face and the thick meat of his jowls quivered.

"You could go over here," he hissed. "I don't give a fuck about your project or the consequences of fighting it. It's not right, and if I end up Project Mushroom's David Kelly, that's fine. But before I go, I need answers."

He dragged the compliant body of Jack Bahram, inch by inch, toward the precipice and hung his head and torso over the drop. He watched the perspiration break on Barham's brow with a certain satisfaction.

"Don't..." he begged.

"Talk and I'll decide," Ashton hissed.

****

"Look, I know it looks insidious, but really, these are desperate times," Barham flapped, flustered. "And there isn't anyone at Medico who isn't under some kind of experimental conditions."

"This is insane," snapped Robert, still pushing the project manager backwards and holding him over the railing. "So you're telling me you're as much a puppet as the people you're experimenting on?"

"More or less," Barham gasped, perspiration running down his face.

"So, the sex buzz that permeates the office..."

"Yes. Everything," Jack said, visibly trembling with fear.

"But why?"

"Medico is heavily subsidised by the government to explore all aspects of mind control," Barham blustered. "We're all contracted to engage on an individual and personal level and to consent to random experimentation as is seen fit. The sexual tension..."

"It's more than tension!" Robert exclaimed. "The office is nothing short of a non-stop orgy!"

"We're fed programmatic drugs through the air-conditioning. We have no control..."

"Really? Or is it just a placebo, and you're simply living out your wildest sexual fantasies in a workplace environment?" Ashton demanded.

Barham shrugged weakly. "I don't know anymore."

"So why haven't I embarked on a lust frenzy?"

"You're the control specimen," Jack said, glancing down at the ground below as the sound of artillery fire began to rent the air. "You were inoculated against it all... as a test of the test."

The sound of heavy engines sounded in the distance, a rumble and grind. It was too dark to make out their source.

"And what about Fay? She doesn't seem to be affected."

"A failed experiment from the early days of the project. Ultimately, she proved to be too neurotic to utilise as a participant, so we wiped her."

The sound of the distant engines swiftly expanded to a roar, and looking out over Jack's arched torso, Robert could make out a line of tanks trundling into the retail park, their caterpillars crushing row upon row of cars, both parked and abandoned, as they drove through the smouldering blockades.

****

Retail Island

It was beginning to rain as the tanks and armoured water cannons rumbled their way across the parked car and into the jostling crowds. Robert marvelled at their indefatigability, the fact they had spent over a fortnight engaged in pointless scuffles and mindless violence over food and clothing – the former of which they could afford, the latter of which they didn't need and were seemingly happy to pay for, but unwilling to grant their fellow humans access to. Both represented extremes of consumerism, but at least in Robert's mind the actions of the former subjects carried some kind of behavioural logic: the survival instinct says to source and secure food supplies. The latter subjects simply made no sense: their mindset centred around an ethos of kill or be killed, to engage in violence without any consideration for one's personal health – for days on end, without so much as consuming food – in order to purchase low-cost fashion clothing they could readily purchase in countless outlets around the country, including the city's high street.

Ashton's thoughts dissipated faster than the knots of rioters when the water cannons began firing high-velocity jets from the directional nozzles attached to their roofs. He had been awake for longer than he could remember now: having barely slept at the hotel, tossing, twitchy and nervous, it had probably been a full week since he had slept for more than four hours on a night, and never once in a single segment. Robert wasn't only aware that his cognitive processes were impaired; he was hyper-aware to the point of paranoia and screaming self-doubt.

****

Back at the hotel room, Fay paced the suite, wringing her hands, chewing her lip, her guts churning with anxiety: she could see that something new was going down at the retail park, but did not have enough of a view to determine precisely what. She had long given her being over to the effects of tempestuous fretting, jittering agitation encroaching so deeply on every corner of her life that, like an advancing army of ants, the worry had inched its way to her core.

Robert wasn't answering his phone, and nor was he picking up or responding to text messages. She couldn't explain why this bothered her so: ultimately, Robert was not her concern, and she didn't feel she knew him well enough to have formed a genuine emotional attachment to him. And yet something pulled in the pit of her stomach, and her concern was heightened by what appeared to be military drones over Ebor Park. The progress they had made towards uncovering Medico's dubious practices had been very much a joint effort, and she felt they made a good team, despite her trepidation over where things were heading.

She had a deep distrust of the slimy, corporate Barham, and she was suspicious of his motives, not only in terms of his involvement in Project Mushroom, but on account of his recent willingness to divulge information about the project – previously considered beyond confidential – to Robert in such a casual and liberal fashion. Was he setting Robert up for a fall? Were his disclosures even true, or was everything a diversion, a smokescreen, a subterfuge?

"Fuckfuckfuck," she muttered under her breath, as she finally gave in to the urge to crack open a can of premixed Gordon's gin and tonic from the minibar.

As the scent of quinine reached her nostrils on the effervescence of the freshly-poured beverage, she saw a flash illuminate the shopping precinct. She froze and caught her breath, and goose pimples immediately prickled her forearms. Another burst of light illuminated the room for an instant, before she saw bright orange flames and a waft of black smoke rise into the foreboding grey sky, with glinting orange sparks carried upwards within. She tensed, and clenched the glass with white knuckles.

****

Robert stood, frozen, perplexed and awed as the tanks rolled across the car park, crushing vehicles which stood in their path. He glanced down at Jack Barham's panic-stricken face, ruddy and pouring with perspiration as he tensed, leaning out over the railing with Robert's fist once again clasping his collar and pushing him forward. The fury had returned on hearing of just how expendable Barham and Medico considered people including its own employees, and he had once again threatened to cast him over the edge and to the ground below.

The fight had gone out of Barham, as he sweated, exhausted with terror, but equally, Robert's own internal conflict dragged back on his spontaneous desire to end Barham's reign by force. Seeing the tanks trundle toward them, Robert knew that, one way or another, the game was over. Ashton slowly released his grip on Barham's collar, the life sapping from his limbs. Jack didn't spring back, and instead hung, limp and dejected-looking. He stood, shaking, and turned, leaning the full weight of his body against the railing as he surveyed the scene below.

"You've done this," Robert hissed.

"I didn't do it on my own," Jack wheezed. "And if you think I chose any of this, you're wrong. I'm just doing a job."

"But how can you live with yourself?"

Jack shook his head slowly. "You really don't understand. We're all guinea pigs at Medico, and there's no free will under Project Mushroom. My conscience has been erased. I feel nothing. But here we are. Changing the world."

The shock of adrenaline returned to Robert's system when the first shot fired from the cannon of the leading tank. The shell ripped from the mouth of the cannon with a booming blast and blew open one side of the expansive plate glass front of the Asda superstore with a shattering crash as shards of glass and other building debris showered onto the crowd in front of it. The gun turret turned a few degrees and fired a second shell, which blew the front out of the other side of the premises. The vibrations violently shook the roof platform on which Robert and Jack stood, and Robert swayed, gripping the railing to help maintain his footing.

Robert had expected the military would have used their force to bring the crowd under control, but now it was anyone's guess as to their strategy. Panic and mayhem broke out as the flames gushed forth from the devastated shop front.

****

Nosnibor

Retail Island

Fay had stopped pacing and had refocused her attention on trawling through the seemingly endless ream of classified files she and Robert had between them managed to gain access. She felt light-headed and her intestines were in turmoil, and she chewed anxiously at the ulcerated interior walls of her cheeks as she read the disturbing catalogue of behaviour-altering drug compounds, and the increasingly inventive – and impossibly deranged – methods of their dissemination. It read in places like a hybrid of Jose Delgado's *Physical Control of the Mind, The Electronic Revolution* by William Burroughs, and Konstantine Raudive's *Breakthrough* – only this was no 'amazing experiment in electronic communication with the dead', but a document of a sustained attempt to reprogramme the living to some kind of reactive zombie status. Some passages were more reminiscent of Krafft-Ebing's *Psychopathia Sexualis*, and it soon became apparent to Fay that the scenarios set out had largely taken place in the office, involving Medico employees, and the interviews transcribed were from the mouths of people she had met, had direct dealings with, and in some instances, worked alongside as colleagues.

She read, jaw agape, about the induction of the local project leaders. Project Mushroom was by no means restricted to Ebor Park or York: Medico had offices and project centres around the globe, and were employing below-board tactics in every single one of them, dispatching experimental chemical cocktails and using advanced – and often unproven – audiovisual technologies, subliminal messaging, and a whole host of unscrupulous, unethical, and seemingly dangerous methodologies.

"I'm surprised they haven't revisited lobotomies and electric shock treatment," Fay muttered to herself, absently chewing the skin by the base of her left thumbnail. She tucked her hair back behind her ear and leaned closer to the screen of the laptop. The bright glow overloaded her retinas. Blinking and squinting slightly, she read about a young, ambitious and slightly rebellious employee at the York office by the name of Jack Barham. She read through page upon page of case notes, reports and transcriptions which detailed his journey, how they had reined him in and essentially turned him. She learned how his apparent immunity to the regular programmes and treatments had been taken as a challenge, and how they had devised and tested more potent blends of drugs and intra-frequency treatments to achieve their objective. Through insidious mind-control and chemical warfare conducted on a targeted, individual basis, a potential mole or whistle-blower of lowly status – Barham was but a data analytics operative at the time – Medico transformed a human being with damaging potential to a trailblazing corporate automaton.

Fay felt the vibrations of two further explosions shake the hotel's structure. She rushed to the window: she still couldn't make out much more than before, only now there was a glowing orange aura above Ebor Park, and the rumbling roar of more helicopters approaching told her things were moving, and fast now. She trembled and feared the worst.

****

Robert and Jack looked in shock and awe as two more tanks, which had been rumbling toward Primark, opened fire and blew the front out of the new store, replicating the scene immediately below them. The crowd's initial reaction was also the same: instead of fighting, they began to flee in all directions in a state of blind panic. But, very swiftly, it became apparent that something had changed. The ruckuses in front of both stored abated, and the blind panic was soon replaced by a strange sense of docile order as the previously rowdy crowds settled.

Robert looked at Jack and Jack looked at Robert.

"What the fuck?" asked Robert, incredulously.

Barham gasped, as if the air was being sucked from his lungs. He turned pale and leaned forward onto the railing, his head hanging down. Robert thought Jack was going to vomit. Barham shook his head. "It's over," he whispered.

"A failed project," Robert said quietly.

"Who's to say? This is not the project, but simply one of its experiments. And there's no success like failure."

"What are you saying?"

"I'm saying that science and experimentation is about learning from your mistakes, and that it's a process of elimination."

"But you said it's over," Ashton pressed.

"For this test, maybe. And also for me... maybe."

Ashton twigged that the sonic waves being pulsed from both Primark and Asda had been disabled as he watched the crowds milling, confused and cattle-like, vacant and exhausted, away from the shops in search of their cars. Some eyed one another suspiciously, but there were no fights, and no indications of aggression. Many hugged and offered other gestures of support. Robert and Jack looked on as the people walked, dazed but seemingly restored to their natural states, toward their cars. Those without cars and those whose cars had been crushed or torched wandered aimlessly, but many received – and accepted – offers of lifts. Robert felt his tension ease and his heart rate reduce as he watched the tanks plough the burned-out hulks of the busses which blockaded the entrances and exits out of the way, and the first cars began to leave.

As the sun began to break through the clouds on the horizon, Robert felt a sense of euphoria, and sensed that the purple and orange tinting of the sky which heralded the arrival of the new day was both literal and symbolic. There were still broken bodies on the tarmac and the retail park bore the scars of the aftermath of brutal devastation, but the beginning of the dawn chorus from the fields and hedgerows beyond gave an indication of hope.

A sudden, single blast of noise cut through his reverie. He immediate recognised the sound as that of a gunshot. He looked around in search of its source, and simultaneously saw Barham slump.

"Jack?" he gasped, superfluously, as the project manager clutched his chest with his right hand and grabbed the railing, white-knuckled with his left.

The air rushed from Barham's lungs as he slid to his knees, a small trickle of blood running from the corner of his mouth and a larger bloom spreading across the front of his shirt around where the chubby, dark-haired hand clutched his chest.

Jack was unable to form words as blood bubbled from his mouth and he fell, silently, to the platform floor. Ashton caught him in time to prevent his dead weight from sliding off the roof and breaking on the hard ground below. He himself felt dizzy, weak, as Barham's weight dragged on him and he laid his body down. The sudden roar of a military helicopter overhead, and the ladder which descended from the hatch open in its side, told him he was saved. And yet, a nagging sense deep within told him this was but a temporary safety, and that he was far from free of Project Mushroom.

From the hotel, Fay saw from her distant vantage, two ant-sized figures being elevated into a military helicopter over on the far side of the retail park. Unaware of the who, what, or why, she felt a wave of anxious nausea punch her in the abdomen.

She could now see cars and vans leaving in a procession that would likely last all day. Part of her knew she should be relieved, but Robert still wasn't answering his phone or picking up her messages. Clenching her fists so that her nails dug into her palms, she feared for the future.

www.ingramcontent.com/pod-product-compliance
Lightning Source LLC
Chambersburg PA
CBHW071311200626
46813CB00015B/1465